W9-ARW-059

# The Swift Boys & Me

KODY KEPLINGER

SCHOLASTIC PRESS | NEW YORK

Library of Congress Cataloging-in-Publication Data

Keplinger, Kody, author.
The Swift boys & me / Kody Keplinger. — First edition.
pages cm
Summary: Nola Sutton has always been friends with the Swift boys, Canaan, Brian, and Kevin, but when their father leaves them without saying good-bye the boys start to change, and her long-time friends begin to pull away from her at a time when she needs them more than ever.
ISBN 978-0-545-56200-3
1. Best friends — Juvenile fiction. 2. Desertion and non-support — Juvenile fiction.
3. Dysfunctional families — Juvenile fiction. 4. Brothers — Juvenile fiction.
[1. Best friends — Fiction. 2. Friendship — Fiction. 3. Family problems — Fiction.
4. Family life — Fiction. 5. Brothers — Fiction.] I. Title. II. Title: Swift boys and me.
PZ7.K439Sw 2014
813.6 — dc23
2013034049

10 9 8 7 6 5 4 3 2 1          14 15 16 17 18

Printed in the U.S.A.          23
First edition, June 2014
Book design by Yaffa Jaskoll

For my hometown:
all the people,
all the places,
all the stories,
and so, so much inspiration.

# Chapter One

I never told the boys I saw their daddy leave that night.

I was outside getting the mail for Mama. I was supposed to check the mailbox when I got off the bus in the afternoon, but it was the last day of sixth grade, and I was so excited to be free for the summer that I'd completely forgot about the mail. It was always just bills, anyway. There was never anything for me except on my birthday or at Christmas, when Mamaw and Papaw sent me cards in brightly colored envelopes. Mama was insistent that I always check the mailbox, though. She said those bills I thought were so boring were important — that's how we kept the lights on.

But I'd forgotten that day, so when she looked on the coffee table and saw there was nothing there, she asked, "Nola Baby, did you get the mail?"

It was late — already past nine — but since it was the last day of school and all, Mama had agreed to let me stay up until eleven. So I was sitting on the couch eating a big bowl of strawberry ice cream and watching Cartoon Network. "Um . . . ," I said. "I think I forgot."

"Well, go check for me now, okay?"

"I'm eating," I whined.

"It takes all of three seconds to go out there, open the box, and come back," she said. "Your ice cream won't melt."

I sighed, all heavy and dramatic — the sigh that always made Mama say things like "Lord help me, I'm about to have a teenager on my hands." She still had eleven months before that happened, though, so I didn't know what she was talking about. What did my sighs have to do with being a teenager? My friend Brian was a teenager, and I never heard him sigh.

I went outside, barefoot, in my T-shirt and shorts. The concrete was warm, even though the sun had set. My teachers in elementary school said that May was still technically spring, but it might as well be summer in

Besser County. It had been in the nineties all week, and even at night the humidity was so bad it made my ponytail frizz into a big brown pouf the second I stepped outside.

Mr. Swift was already in his car with the engine running as I made my way down the driveway. Even though we lived in a duplex — which is basically two houses smushed together into one, but separated by a wall on the inside so two families could live there — we didn't share a driveway. Mama and I had one leading to our side of the house and the Swifts had one leading to theirs. But they were still close enough to each other, only our front walks and some grass between them. Mr. Swift started backing down his driveway just as I opened the mailbox.

There was nothing in it, so it had been a wasted trip. I shut the little door and looked up. Mr. Swift's car — a silver Saturn — was turning onto the road. I figured he was running an errand, like going to the grocery or the hardware store or something. I guess I should have realized that most places were already closed. Our tiny little town shut down at about eight every night. But I didn't think much of it, seeing him leaving.

I waved.

And he waved back.

I found out later that was more of a good-bye than his boys ever got.

*   *   *

Everything had been fine earlier that day. Canaan and I had been whooping and hollering when we got off the bus. Kevin was behind us, jabbering about something. Kevin was *always* jabbering about something. Brian hadn't ridden the bus home, though. Middle school graduation was earlier that day. Anyway, we'd gotten out of class to watch the ceremony, which didn't involve ugly caps and gowns like the high school graduation did. Afterwards, Brian had gone home with his friend Ty, who was having some party for all the graduating eighth graders at his house.

"Hey," Canaan said to Kevin and me as the bus pulled away. "Did you notice Teddy Ryan wasn't on the bus today?"

All three of us automatically looked down the street toward Teddy Ryan's house. His parents' car wasn't in the driveway.

"Can we?" Kevin asked, bouncing up and down beside me. He was short for a third grader. Even on his tiptoes, the top of his head barely reached my chin. "Please? Can we? Can we?"

"I don't know," I said, glancing at Canaan. "What about looking for jobs?"

The boys and I had a lot of saving to do that summer. Mama had said she'd take us to Wheaton Brothers Traveling Circus at the beginning of August, but only if we could earn the money to pay for our own tickets. It was the first time the circus had come anywhere near our town in five years, and we *had* to go. Our parents had taken us the last time, when Canaan and me were seven, and it had been amazing, the best time the boys and I had ever had together. We'd even gotten to ride a real elephant. Kevin was too little to remember it all, which was just more reason to go this year.

Tickets were forty dollars apiece, though. It would take a lot of lawn mowing and dog walking to earn that much over the summer. We needed to start setting up jobs now.

"We can do that tomorrow," Canaan said, wiping

sweat off his forehead. The ends of his light brown hair were wet and curling around his face. "We got time."

"Well . . . all right. But we have to start first thing."

"We will." Canaan grinned at me. He had a little gap between his two front teeth that always made me want to smile back at him. "Let's dump our stuff inside. We'll meet back here in five minutes."

"Yes, yes, yes!" Kevin cheered as he and Canaan took off running for their front door.

I pulled my house key out of my back pocket. Mama wouldn't be home for a few hours. It was all right, though. The boys' mama, Mrs. Swift, always checked in on me. She wasn't quite a babysitter — I was no baby — but sometimes it was nice knowing there was a grown-up next door if I needed anything while Mama was at work.

I tossed my backpack in my room and grabbed three Popsicles from the freezer. When I went back outside to meet Canaan and Kevin, I gave each of them one.

"Blue!" Kevin said. "That's my favorite color, you know. All the best things are blue. The ocean. The sky. Luke Skywalker's lightsaber. Have you seen *Star Wars* yet, Nola? Daddy made me watch all of them. They're my favorite movies."

"We know," Canaan said. "You tell us every day."

Kevin was eight. Being so much younger than us, I know Canaan wanted to ditch him most of the time. Especially because Kevin had a habit of talking way too much and repeating himself. But I liked him. It was hard not to smile when you were around someone like Kevin. Well, at least for me. I think siblings are excluded from that rule. Not that I'd know. I'm an only child.

After we finished our Popsicles, Canaan led the way through three of our neighbors' backyards, darting around bushes and behind swing sets until we reached the wooden fence around the Ryans' yard.

We didn't like the Ryans too much. They moved into the subdivision three years ago, and the first thing they did was build a fence. No one else had a fence. We all played in each others' backyards. We drew on each others' sidewalks with colored chalk and used each others' jungle gyms. No one seemed to care. But I guess the Ryans cared because they put up a fence, and then a trampoline.

They were the only family in the subdivision with a trampoline. And I think every kid in the neighborhood was jealous.

Canaan and I tried to make friends with their son, Teddy, at first. We figured if we were friends with him, he'd let us in the fence to play on his trampoline. But Teddy was kinda weird. He was only a year younger than Canaan and me, but you'd think he was much younger by the way he acted. We'd caught him picking his nose a few times, and he was always staring at us. A couple months ago he stuck gum in my hair on the bus. I cried when Mama had to cut it out. I'd been wanting to grow my hair long forever, but thanks to Teddy Ryan, it was above my shoulders again.

So the whole idea of being friends with him hadn't worked out so well.

But that was okay because we had another way to play on his trampoline. Couple years ago, we found a loose board in their fence. You had to know exactly where it was, but if you could find it, and you pushed on it, it would swing up. There was just enough space for Canaan, Kevin, and me to crawl through, one at a time. Not Brian, though. He'd gotten too big in the last year or so. His shoulders always got stuck now.

Every time we saw that Teddy and his parents weren't home, we'd sneak over and push the loose board. We never told none of the other kids in the neighborhood about it. Not even our friend Felicia. It was our little secret, the boys' and mine.

Canaan ran his hand across the fence planks until he found the right one. He pushed and it swung up. He let me crawl through first, then Kevin, before he followed.

"What should we play?" I asked, hoisting myself onto the trampoline, then holding out a hand to help Kevin up.

"Popcorn!" Kevin exclaimed. "Please, please, please Popcorn. I love Popcorn. The food *and* the game, but since we're on the trampoline, I mean the game. Can we please play Popcorn?"

"All right," Canaan groaned, climbing onto the trampoline with us. He was tall — the tallest boy in our class — so it was a piece of cake for him. "We get it — Popcorn. But Nola gets to be the kernel first."

"Why?" Kevin asked.

"Because you always go first," I said, tapping him playfully on the top of the head. His blond hair was sticking up in every direction. He had too much of it to even bother keeping it neat. It wasn't that it was long. It was just real thick, like his mama's.

He grinned at me. "Okay. But I'm next."

I crawled to the center of the trampoline and sat down, wrapping my arms around my knees as tight as I could, making myself into a little ball.

"Ready?" Canaan asked. He and Kevin were standing on opposite sides of me.

"Ready," I said.

Then the boys started jumping and I started bouncing. I laughed, my hands gripping my elbows. I was determined to last as long as I could. Once I popped, it would be Canaan's or Kevin's turn. I could go again in a few minutes, but I was determined to beat my record.

"One . . . two . . . three . . . ," Canaan and Kevin shouted with each bounce.

The longest I'd ever lasted was fifteen bounces. It was pathetic compared to Canaan, who could go all the way up to thirty. But it seemed like Canaan was the best at everything he tried. He'd been the fastest boy in the sixth grade, he was always the last one standing when our gym teacher made us play dodgeball, and when we played basketball with some of the other kids in the neighborhood, he always won, even though there were older kids who played, too.

Not like me. I was short and a little on the chubby side, definitely not too athletic. But Canaan didn't seem to notice. He still picked me first for his team, whatever game we were playing. He didn't mind if I slowed him down.

"... ten ... eleven ..."

I started laughing with my face pressed against my knees. It was a nervous laugh, though. I was so close to my record, but Canaan and Kevin were jumping higher and higher, tossing me around in the middle of the trampoline.

I ended up popping at thirteen.

"Shoot," I groaned, throwing myself onto my back as the boys quit jumping.

"You'll get it next time, Nola," Kevin said. "Now move. It's my turn."

"Say 'please,' Kevin," Canaan scolded. "You know Mama doesn't like it when you're bossy."

This made me snort out loud. "You're one to talk. You're about the bossiest person I know, Canaan Swift."

"Yeah, but he's eight," Canaan said. "It's different."

"Whatever you say." I sat up and got to my feet, letting Kevin take his place in the middle.

We played for a couple of hours, but I never beat my record. Canaan made it all the way up to forty bounces, though. Then, all too soon, Kevin froze. "Alert! Alert!" he said in a robot voice. The Ryans' car was pulling into their driveway.

"Uh-oh," Canaan said, jumping off the trampoline and landing in a crouch. "Come on, y'all. We better hurry."

Kevin and I scrambled down and ran for the fence. Once we were through, we stayed close to the planks, holding our breath. The Ryans were carrying in groceries, and we had to wait until they were inside before we could move, or else they'd spot us running out of their yard.

When their front door finally shut for good, Canaan whispered, "Go!"

We took off back across our neighbors' lawns, laughing as we ran. Canaan had to slow down so Kevin and me could keep up.

When we got back to the duplex, Mrs. Swift was sitting in a folding chair in the backyard, drinking sweet tea from a mason jar and reading a magazine. She looked up at us and smiled as we came to a stop in front of her, panting like thirsty dogs. "Where've y'all been?" she asked.

"Down the street," Canaan said. She didn't know we snuck into the Ryans' yard. Whenever we told our parents "down the street," they just figured we were playing with some of the other kids in the subdivision. There were lots of us, after all.

"Is Brian back?" I asked.

"Yep. Just picked him up from Ty's. He's inside." She held up a hand, stopping us before we could take off for the front door. "Wait, wait. Canaan, you need to clean your room."

"I will."

"No, you need to clean it now. I know if I let you wait until this evening, you'll put it off until it's time for bed."

"I won't."

"You always do," Kevin chimed. "Mama told you to clean it yesterday, remember? But you said you'd just act like you had other stuff to do until it was bedtime and then —"

I planted a hand over Kevin's mouth. The look on Canaan's face made me think he might try to kill his brother in a minute.

Mrs. Swift just grinned, though. She had the same red cheeks and giant smile as Kevin. "Clean your room, Canaan," she said. "Nola can stay for an hour. After that, you need to get to work. It's starting to stink in there."

She wasn't lying, either. Once we were inside, we headed straight for Kevin and Canaan's room. It smelled like a mix of popcorn and dirty clothes. But they didn't seem bothered by it.

Brian had his own room, but it was tiny, and the Xbox was in his little brothers' room, so he was in there most of the time, anyway. Right then, he was sitting on the floor with a controller in his hand. He looked up when we came in. "Hey," he said, reaching up to adjust his glasses.

"How was the party?" I asked, sitting down on the carpet next to him.

"All right," he said. "Loud, though. I don't see the point in having music so loud you can't hear other people talking to you. It kind of gave me a headache."

"Were there girls?" Canaan asked, plopping down on his bed. Kevin sat next to him.

"Yeah."

"Did you kiss any of them?" Kevin asked. Lately, he'd been obsessed with kissing. He'd been asking everyone who they'd kissed and where and why. Last week, he asked me if I'd ever kissed Canaan. Of course we hadn't, but I had to admit, all his kissing questions had me thinking about that kinda stuff, too.

I looked at Brian, really staring at his face. Had he ever kissed a girl? Would I be able to tell if he had? Like, would he look different somehow? Right now, he mostly just looked like Canaan — tall with long arms and legs, light brown hair, and green eyes. Only he had glasses and no gap between his teeth. If he kissed a girl, would he suddenly start looking older? Would he get a mustache like Mr. Swift?

The thing is, I knew he'd tell me if he had. Even if he didn't tell Canaan and Kevin. At least, he would if I asked. Brian didn't get embarrassed easily or upset about much. I knew I could always ask him questions about older kids, even about personal stuff. Like kissing.

"No," he said. "I didn't kiss anyone."

"Why not?" Kevin asked. "Did none of them wanna kiss you?"

"Stop being weird," Canaan said. "Hey, Brian, can you put in another game? Nola can only stay another hour, so let's play something where we all get a turn."

Brian passed me the other controller and switched the game. We played for a while, just sitting around laughing and talking. I lost every single game we played, but I didn't really care. I never did. I was just happy to be with them, even in Canaan's smelly room.

That's how I expected the whole summer to be. It's how every summer before had been. Me and the Swift brothers spent every day together. We were always playing and laughing. Only this summer would be even better because we'd go to the circus before school started, just like we had when we were little. All of our summers were great, but this would be the best we'd ever had.

I had no idea that later that night, when I watched Mr. Swift pull out of the driveway, it meant everything was about to change. Forever.

# Two Summers Ago

*Canaan and me were sitting on my front steps when two boys who lived down the street, Andy and Peter, pulled up on their bikes, hollering at us. Well, just at Canaan.*

*"We're gonna play kickball at the playground," Peter yelled. "You wanna come?"*

*"Sure." Canaan stood up and hopped down the steps. "Come on, Nola."*

*I was about to stand up when Andy groaned. "Not her. She ain't no good. And she's slow. She can stay here."*

*I bit my lip and tried not to cry. I cried too easy, and it wasn't like this was anything new. Andy and Peter had always been mean boys. The kind who pushed the littler kids around and knocked over swing sets at night. I sat back down and wrapped my arms around my knees.*

*"I ain't going if Nola can't come," Canaan said, sitting right back down beside me.*

*"Why?" Peter asked. "She your girlfriend?" He and Andy started singing as they rode away. "Canaan and Nola, sitting in a tree, K-I-S-S-I-N-G."*

*"You don't gotta stay," I told Canaan. "If you wanna go, you can."*

But he shook his head. "I don't go nowhere you can't go. Besides, it wouldn't have been fun without you there. I'd rather stay here."

"You're just saying that."

"Am not. I mean it. You're way more fun than they are. That's why you're my best friend. And why I ain't going with them if you're not invited."

I couldn't help smiling. "Thanks, Canaan."

He shrugged, like it was nothing at all. Then he grabbed my hand and stood up, pulling me along with him. "Now come on. Let's go see if Mrs. Santos will let us play with her dog."

"All right."

We took off running down the street, and even though I couldn't keep up with him, he didn't mind slowing down, just as long as we could stick together.

# Chapter Two

I had no idea anything was wrong at the Swifts' until the next day when I knocked on the door and Brian answered.

"Hey," I said. "I'm about to ride my bike up to Rocky's for a milkshake. Do y'all want to come? I figure we can go around looking for jobs after."

"Not today, Nola," he said. His voice sounded pained, and it wasn't until then that I noticed how bad he looked. He had big, dark circles under his eyes, and his shoulders were slumped forward. Like his bones just couldn't take the weight.

Inside the house, I could hear somebody crying.

"What's going on?" I asked.

"Just come back another day —"

"No." Then Canaan was there, standing in the door-way next to his brother. He didn't look great, either, but not as bad as Brian. His light brown hair hadn't been combed, but that was normal. His eyes were red, like he hadn't slept well. "I'll go with you, Nola."

"Canaan," Brian said. "Don't you think you should stay here today?"

He didn't answer as he pushed past Brian and went to get his bike, which was always leaning against the side of the duplex.

Brian didn't move. He chewed on his lip and adjusted his glasses. "Canaan," he said. "You ought to stay here. Mama needs us. And Kevin —"

"They're making a big deal out of nothing," Canaan snapped, rolling his bike over to me. "He's coming back, Brian. If he wasn't, he'd have said good-bye."

"But —"

"Just shut up, all right?" Canaan yelled. "Shut up and go inside if you're so worried about them!"

I cringed. I'd never heard Canaan yell at Brian like that. It was the kinda yelling he usually saved for Andy and Peter. Not his own brothers.

"Come on, Nola," Canaan said, kicking off the ground and starting to pedal down the street.

I glanced back at Brian. "I . . . I guess I'll see you later."

He didn't say anything. He just turned around and walked inside, slamming the door behind him.

I hoped he wasn't mad at me. I hadn't meant to start a fight. Something was obviously wrong, though, by the way Brian talked about Kevin and their mama. I wanted to know what was going on, but I was afraid to ask. I'd never seen Brian or Canaan like this.

I took off after Canaan, catching up with him on the corner. We turned left toward Rocky's, the local burger and fries restaurant. The hamburgers were usually burnt and the fries were soggy, but they made great milkshakes, and the weatherman said it was already ninety-five degrees out. It felt hotter.

We leaned our bikes up next to the restaurant's front door. It didn't look like there were too many people inside — there never were. Most people used the drive-through, but I liked to sit down inside. Plus, they always had the radio on my favorite country station, Outlaw 104, which was real nice.

"Hello, hello!" Edna Forman, the manager, called

when we walked inside. "Two of my favorite kids in town. Where are your brothers, Canaan? They didn't want to see me today?"

Canaan shrugged. "Guess not."

"Well," Edna huffed. "I guess we'll have to make them regret that, won't we?" She grinned, showing off a few of her missing teeth, and tapped the counter. "Y'all get up here and tell me what I can get for you."

"Peanut-butter milkshake, please," I told her.

"Chocolate," Canaan said.

I started to reach in my pocket and pull out the money Mama had left me for lunch, but Edna waved her hand. "Don't even worry about it," she said. "This one's on the house."

"You sure?" I asked.

"Yesterday was the last day of school, right? And y'all both passed? I think that deserves a free milkshake." She looked at Canaan and winked. "That'll teach your brothers to not come see me."

"Thanks, Edna," I said.

Canaan and me found seats at a sticky table. He still wasn't saying much, and I felt kinda silly, just sitting there, not talking, with nothing to do. So I hummed along with an old Garth Brooks song that was on the radio. It was one Mama always loved. After about a minute, Canaan sighed, real loud.

"I know you wanna ask," he said.

"Ask what?"

"Don't be dumb, Nola," he said. "You heard me and Brian. I know you wanna know what's going on."

"You don't gotta tell me if you don't want," I said, but of course I was dying to know. I was sure he'd tell me, though, no matter what I said. Canaan always told me everything. Just like I told him everything.

All three of the Swift boys were my best friends, but Canaan was my best-best friend. We were the same age — our birthdays were only three weeks apart — and since my last name was Sutton, which also started with an S, we always sat together in class and had lockers right next to each other. You couldn't pull Canaan and me apart if you wanted to.

He chewed on his bottom lip — all three of the boys did that when they were nervous. After a minute he said, "Mama got into a fight with Dad last night. Kevin and I were playing video games in my room, and we could hear them yelling at each other."

That wasn't all too surprising, really. Mr. and Mrs. Swift argued a lot. I could hear them yelling at each other through the wall that separated their side of the duplex from mine. It happened a few times a month. Mama always turned up the radio or turned on the faucet to hide the sound. She said it was rude to eavesdrop, even if we really weren't trying to. I didn't mind. It was better than hearing them yell, which made me upset even if I wasn't in the house with them.

I'd had the cartoons on loud last night. Maybe that's why I hadn't heard them.

"What were they fighting about?" I asked.

Canaan shrugged. "I don't know. I never ask."

I nodded. Sometimes, Mama and her boyfriend, Richard, would get into arguments. They didn't yell like Mr. and Mrs. Swift, at least not very often, but even when they did, I didn't ever want to know what they were fighting over. I was always too scared it was my fault, even when I hadn't done anything wrong. I worried about stuff like that a lot, though. Not just with my parents, but with everyone. Mama said I had enough worry in me for the whole town. She said it's all Grandma

Lucy's fault because she used to babysit me when I was little, and she was always yelling. She yelled at everyone and everything. Even me. I don't really remember all too well — I was only about three or four — but I sure hated yelling or getting in trouble or having anybody mad at me. It always made me feel sick to my stomach.

"I turned the TV volume up real high, though," Canaan went on. "Because Kevin always gets upset when they holler at each other, so I turned it up so he couldn't hear. Then I heard the doors slamming. When I walked out of my room a little while later, Mama was already in bed, and Dad's car wasn't in the driveway."

I was about to tell him that I'd seen Mr. Swift leave last night and had even waved, but before I could, Edna was standing there with our milkshakes. Her pale, pale skin and silvery hair made her look a little like a ghost hovering next to our table.

"Here you go," she said, handing me my peanut-butter shake. "And for you, Canaan. You kids enjoy, all right? Let me know if you need anything."

"We will," I said. "Thank you again, Edna."

"Anytime, sweetheart."

Canaan sipped from his chocolate shake for a minute. He didn't start talking again until Edna was back across the room.

"Mama has been crying all day," he told me, his voice lower than before. I had to lean on the table, craning my neck toward him, to hear. "She keeps saying he's left us. Like, forever."

"Oh," I said because I wasn't sure what you're supposed to say when someone tells you something like that.

"And now Kevin is hiding in our closet and he won't come out, and Brian is acting like he's the boss or something. It's so stupid. He's coming back."

"He is?"

Canaan glared at me. "Of course he is. He wouldn't just leave without saying good-bye to us. He'll probably come back tonight even. Dads don't just leave like that."

I'd have to take his word for it. I never knew my daddy. He died in a coal mining accident before I was even a year old. Mama never told me the details. I don't think she liked talking about it. She just said he was a good man and a good daddy and that I was lucky to have had him for those seven months I can't even remember.

Canaan knew more about having a daddy than I did, so if he said they didn't just leave forever without saying good-bye, I believed him. It did seem like a weird thing to do. Even though I'd lived next door my whole life, I didn't know Mr. Swift real well because he worked a lot and wasn't home that much. When I did talk to him, he seemed nice enough, even if he never said much — at least not when I was around. He had Canaan's gap-toothed smile and Brian's pug nose and the same green eyes all the boys shared. He reminded me a lot of the boys, actually. And none of them would do something like that, so he wouldn't, either.

Canaan had to be right. Mrs. Swift and Kevin and Brian were just overreacting.

"He will," I said. "He will come back."

"I know," Canaan said. "I wish they'd quit acting stupid about it."

We finished our milkshakes and said good-bye to Edna, then we rode our bikes back to the subdivision. "You still wanna look for jobs?" I asked. Canaan nodded, so we started riding around the block, stopping in to ask some of our neighbors if they needed any work done and letting them know our fees. We got a few good leads, and Mr. Fisk even told us to come back next Wednesday to wash his car. It was a good start.

On our way back to the duplex, we stopped at Felicia Hooper's house. She was outside playing with the new yellow Labrador puppy her parents had bought her for fifth-grade graduation.

"He's cute, right?" Felicia said as the puppy jumped up and down at our feet, scratching at our bare legs. "His name is Jabberwocky, but we just call him JW for short."

"Hey, JW," I said, leaning down to scratch behind the puppy's floppy yellow ears. "You're a sweetie, aren't you?"

"He doesn't do tricks yet," Felicia said, rubbing a smudge of dirt off her dark brown cheek. "But we're going to teach him lots of them when he's a little bigger."

"Ain't he adorable, Canaan?" I asked.

Canaan shrugged. I was surprised by how quiet he was being. He'd begged his parents for a dog for years. He loved them. I figured he'd be trying to hog JW for himself. A puppy was even better than Teddy Ryan's trampoline.

"If you ever need someone to walk him, let us know," I told Felicia. "We're not too expensive."

"I think Mama expects me to walk him myself," Felicia said. "But I'll let you know."

"Felicia!" Mrs. Hooper poked her head out the kitchen window. "Honey, come inside and help me set the table."

"Do I *have* to?" Felicia asked.

"Yes you do, missy."

"Fine." She bent down and scooped up JW. "Y'all can come by and play with him whenever you want." She smiled, showing off her multicolored braces. "We're getting a grill, too, so Mama says we can have friends over for burgers this summer."

"That'd be nice," I said. "We'll definitely come by. See you later, Felicia."

Canaan and me pushed our bikes across the street, toward the duplex. It was almost dinnertime, and both Mama's and Richard's cars were in our driveway. Mr. Swift's Saturn still wasn't in theirs, though. We put our bikes on the side of the house. I could tell Canaan was dragging his feet as we headed to our front doors.

"You don't wanna go home yet, do you?"

Canaan folded his arms over his chest and kicked at the grass. "I just don't wanna listen to them say mean things about Dad," he said. "Mama and Brian are both going to complain about him because they don't think he's coming back. And they're wrong. And I don't feel like hearing it."

"Well, you can have dinner with us," I said. "Mama's making quesadillas."

"Okay," Canaan said. "That sounds good."

I didn't even bother asking Mama if it was okay. Half the time, she just assumed one of the boys was eating with us. So when Canaan and me walked inside, she barely even noticed. "Hey, kids," she said from the kitchen.

"Where's Richard?" I asked.

"Right here!"

I shrieked as Richard came up behind me and started tickling my sides. I howled and wiggled, trying to get away. After half a minute, he let me go, laughing.

"I'll get you back for that," I said, turning to face him. I had to crane my neck to look at him. Richard was about the tallest man I'd ever seen. He had to duck a little to go through doorways in our house, even.

"I'd like to see you try, kiddo."

I stuck my tongue out at him.

Richard stuck his out at me, too, then turned to Canaan. "C. Swift! How you been?"

Canaan shrugged. He'd been doing an awful lot of shrugging today.

"Glad to be out of school?"

He nodded, but he still didn't say nothing.

Richard looked at me. A *what's up with him?* kinda look, but I just turned away, pretending I didn't see. Canaan didn't seem like he wanted to talk about his daddy, so I wouldn't talk about it, neither.

"There's enough for everyone, right, Mama?"

"Sure is," she said, pulling some plates from the cabinets. She had to stand on tiptoe to reach them. Unlike Richard, she was kinda short. She said the women in our family never got taller than five two, and I was almost there.

"Good." I turned to Canaan. "Should you let your mama know you're eating over here tonight?"

"She can probably guess where I'm at," Canaan said.

"That's true," Mama interjected. "But it's still nice to let her know. Nola Baby, why don't you give her a call.

"Okay," I said, shooting a glance at Canaan. He just shrugged again. It was really starting to get annoying.

After two rings, Brian answered. "Hello?"

"Hey, Brian. It's Nola. Mama wanted me to tell y'all that Canaan's eating over here tonight."

There was a long pause, and for a minute I thought maybe we'd gotten disconnected. Then Brian said, "Can you put him on the phone?"

I looked over my shoulder at Canaan. I mouthed, *Brian wants to talk to you.* But he shook his head.

I cleared my throat. "Um, he's busy," I said. "And we're about to eat, so I better go."

"Nola." Brian's voice was soft, steady, the way it always was. But he sounded sad, too. Sad, but like he was trying not to let it show. "I don't know what Canaan told you, but things aren't real good over here. He needs to be here with us. You understand, right?"

"I . . ." I glanced back again, but Canaan just kept shaking his head. "I gotta go. Canaan will be home later, okay? Bye, Brian."

I hung up before he could say anything else, but I felt real bad about it. If Brian wasn't mad at me before, he probably was now. It made my stomach hurt to think about. But Canaan was right. Brian was just being stupid about the whole thing. Mr. Swift would probably be home before we even finished eating dinner. He shouldn't be trying to make Canaan feel bad over something so dumb.

"Dinner's ready," Mama said, carrying over the plates, piled high with extra-cheesy quesadillas.

We all sat down at our tiny table to eat. After we said grace, Richard and Mama did most of the talking, and I piped up every once in a while, but Canaan didn't hardly say a word. Mama asked him once or twice if he was feeling okay, and he said yes and shrugged, *again*, but that was all. He did eat everything on his plate, though. I think that made her feel better.

After the plates were cleared, I walked Canaan outside. He started chewing on his lip again, and he shoved his hands into his pockets. "I guess it's time, huh?"

"To go home?"

"Yeah." He groaned. "I wish Dad would hurry up and get home already. The longer he takes, the worse it's gonna get. Kevin's probably still locked in the closet."

I imagined tiny little Kevin in the boys' dark closet, curled up into a ball on the floor. The thought made me want to cry. I swallowed. "Your daddy will be home soon."

"Yeah, I know. Anyway, thanks for dinner. Tell your mama it was really good."

"I will."

He sighed. "All right, well . . . see you tomorrow, Nola."

If I'd known then that that night would be one of the last times Canaan Swift was ever in my house, I would have stopped him. I wouldn't have let him leave. I would have asked Mama if Canaan could stay the night, sleep on the couch. I would have held on as long as I could.

I wouldn't have let him walk away, watching from the sidewalk until he was inside his house and the door had closed behind him.

If I'd known, maybe things would've been different.

# Chapter Three

A few days later, Mr. Swift still hadn't come back. I'd sit next to the living room window, the one that looked out at the street, and watch for his Saturn, expecting it to pull up at any minute.

I didn't see the boys much during those days, but I figured that was because I hadn't left the house much. I'd woken up the morning after Canaan ate with us with a stuffy nose and a cough. Mama kept me inside, pouring orange juice and chicken noodle soup down my throat. When she was at work, Richard would drop by to make sure I was all right. He was the boss where he worked, so he was able to get away for a few minutes to bring by magazines, movies, or new colored pencils for drawing to keep me from getting bored.

At night, in my room, I'd tap on the wall next to my bed. Canaan's bed was on the other side, and when we were six, we'd made up a code. One tap was "hi." Two fast taps was "good night." Then there were different rhythms and patterns that meant other things. We couldn't have whole conversations or anything, but it was a good way to pass the time when neither of us could sleep.

For two nights, I tapped on the wall and Canaan tapped back.

On the third night, he didn't reply.

When I finally got over my cold, I went back outside, expecting the boys to be there waiting for me. But they weren't. I looked in the backyard. I looked on Teddy Ryan's trampoline. I rode my bike to Rocky's and to the playground and to Felicia's, thinking maybe they'd gone to play with her puppy. It wasn't like them to not be outside in the summer. But I was too scared to knock on their front door after last time. What if Brian and Canaan got in a fight again? What if they were mad at *me* for some reason?

I did work up the nerve to call their house once, but nobody answered the phone.

I waited for them to come outside for two days. Then, Wednesday morning, I walked out into the backyard and found Kevin sitting on the swing set. He wasn't swinging, just sitting and staring at the back of the duplex.

"Hey," I said, running toward him. "Where you been? Feels like I ain't seen y'all in forever. Where's Brian and Canaan?"

Kevin didn't say anything.

"Hey, didn't you hear me?" I asked, sitting down on the swing beside his. "I asked where y'all have been. Did you get sick, too?"

He didn't even look at me. He didn't move.

"Kevin?" I said, reaching out to put a hand on his shoulder.

"Don't bother."

I looked up. Canaan was walking around the side of the house, his arms crossed over his dirty-looking T-shirt. His eyes were narrowed and sharp. Like he was mad. Madder than I'd ever seen him.

"He doesn't talk no more," Canaan said, but he wasn't

looking at me. He was staring at Kevin. "Ain't said a word in days. He's being a big baby."

"Canaan."

"Well, he is!" Canaan snapped. "He don't shut up a day in his life, then Dad's gone a couple days and he acts like it's the end of the world. They all do. No one believes he's coming back."

"I do," I told him.

Canaan's shoulders eased and his face relaxed. It was like watching his whole body bend, like a flower wilting in a vase. But he didn't say another word to me. He just kept looking at Kevin. This time when he spoke, his voice was quieter and not as harsh. "Brian's riding his bike to the store. Do you want anything?"

Kevin shook his head.

"Fine." Canaan turned and started walking back around the house again.

"Wait," I said, running to catch up with him. "Are you okay?"

"Yeah," he said. "Just ticked off."

"I don't blame you. It's gotta be annoying, having them all act like that about your daddy." I started to reach for his hand, the way we always did when one of us was upset, but he pulled away, folding his arms over his chest again. I shoved my hands in the pockets of my shorts instead, pretending like nothing had just happened. "We've gotta wash Mr. Fisk's car today, you know. He said we ought to be there around three."

"I don't feel like it," Canaan said.

"But we promised him. And we've gotta start saving now or —"

"Can you do it without me?" he asked. "Sorry. I'll help with the next one. I just wanna be alone. I'm sick of being around people."

"Even me?"

We reached the side of the duplex, where our bikes were leaning against the wall. He grabbed his and started wheeling it toward the sidewalk. I followed, but he didn't really answer me. After a minute, he just said, "I need to be alone today."

"Um, okay. But I'll see you tomorrow?"

"Yeah."

He took off in the direction of the playground. I just stood there, watching him ride off, feeling disappointed. After being inside for a few days, I'd expected all the boys to be waiting for me to get better, ready to start working on our summer plans. They didn't seem to want me around at all, though.

I walked back around the house, where Kevin was still sitting on the swing. I sat beside him again, using my foot to push my swing back and forth. I'd never been with Kevin for more than thirty seconds without him saying something. It was scary and strange for him to be so quiet.

I couldn't help remembering when he used to roar. Literally. The boys and I would walk down the hill behind the subdivision, into the patch of woods. We'd pretend it was a jungle. Sometimes, Brian, Canaan, and me were explorers. Sometimes, we'd have been on a plane that had crashed there. But no matter what we were, Kevin was always a lion.

He'd lurk behind trees, growling and roaring at us before running off in the opposite direction. Then, when we weren't looking, he'd pounce on us. He'd always get really into the role. Even when me and the other boys got hungry and decided to head back to the house for lunch, he'd only follow us on all fours, roaring instead of talking.

I wished he'd roar now. At least I'd know he could still make a sound.

"There are lions at the circus, you know," I said. "Big ones *and* baby ones. You got to pet one of the baby ones last time, but you probably don't remember. Do you?"

Kevin just shook his head.

"Maybe you'll get to pet one again. Wouldn't that be cool? The circus is amazing, Kevin. I can't wait for you to see it. There are so many animals. And people who walk on wires. I bet you can't wait, can you?"

Silence. He didn't nod or shake his head or shrug or nothing. Just stared straight ahead.

"Come on, Kevin," I said. "Your daddy's coming back. I promise. Canaan knows it, too. Biting your tongue won't help none. You might as well talk to me."

Kevin lowered his head. I could see a few tears on his face then, which made me feel real bad. I slid off my swing and knelt down beside him, wrapping my arms around him. He leaned his head on my shoulder, his thick blond hair getting in my face.

"Shh," I murmured, the way Mama did when I was upset. But there was no point. Even Kevin's crying was quiet.

I just sat there, stroking his head for a while. But it didn't feel like Kevin anymore. It felt like another boy I was hugging. Like a stranger. I believed he'd come back, though. Just like Mr. Swift. They'd both come back soon, and Canaan would stop being mad and Brian would stop looking so sad and this summer — our best summer ever — would go back to being the way it was supposed to.

I hugged Kevin closer and told him what I kept trying to tell myself. "It'll all get better soon."

# Chapter Four

But a few days went by, and it still wasn't getting better, as far as I could tell. Kevin still wouldn't talk. He just sat in the backyard — if he came out of the house at all — and stared at nothing. I didn't see Canaan much. Every time I knocked on the door, Brian said he was either already gone or asleep. And even though I told him they were all welcome over for dinner, they never came.

I had plenty to keep me busy, though. Without Canaan's help, the jobs we'd signed up for took twice as long. Most days, I left the house around ten in the morning and didn't get back inside until dinnertime.

"It's awful hot out, Nola," Mrs. Santos said, bringing me a glass of lemonade while I took a break from mowing her yard. "Why don't you go on home and come back tomorrow? I'm worried you'll get heatstroke out here."

"I'm all right," I said, even though my T-shirt was soaked with sweat. Mama said it was supposed to get up past a hundred degrees today. I drank all the lemonade in one gulp.

"You sure?" she asked. "I didn't know you'd be doing all this by yourself. Wasn't Canaan supposed to help you?"

"He ain't feeling well."

It wasn't exactly a lie.

She took the glass from me with a sigh. "Well, if you're sure you'll be fine . . ."

"I will be, Mrs. Santos. I promise. If I feel sick, I'll stop."

"You better. Your mama will kill me if anything happens to you." She reached out and squeezed my shoulder. "Let me know if you need anything else."

"I will."

I was on my way home that evening, tired and ready for dinner, when Mr. Briggs hollered at me. He was sitting on his front porch, barefoot, whittling a block of wood.

"I hear you and the Swift boys are trying to earn some money," he said, his voice deep and gravelly like rocks by the riverbank.

Mr. Briggs was old. The oldest man I'd ever met. Mama said he was old even when she was a kid. He was sort of a town legend, too. Mama told me he fought in World War II. And that he was the first black man to serve on town council back in the seventies. Nowadays, though, he mostly just sat on his porch, whittling these pretty little things. We had a few of his carvings in our house, actually. He sent them to every house in the subdivision at Christmas. Last year, he sent Mama and me a little statue of baby Jesus in the manger.

"Yes, sir. We are," I said.

Carefully, he put down his knife. "Well, I might have a job if y'all want it."

"Sure. What can we do for you?"

"I've got a bunch of these little trinkets here. I need to get them to some people around town. Would y'all mind delivering them? I've got about twenty, and I'd be willing to pay."

"Are you selling them now?"

"Nah. I just make them for fun, and if people want them, I'll give them. But they're not worth nothing."

"That ain't true. They're real good, sir."

"You're a sweetheart. But I'm not sure I'd feel right taking money for them."

"Well, then are you sure you wanna pay us to deliver them? If you're not making money off them —"

"Don't you worry about that. I can pay you and the boys. Come back tomorrow and I'll write down the names of all the people who asked for one of my little carvings."

"All right. I'll tell the boys. Thanks, Mr. Briggs."

He just nodded and smiled and went back to his whittling.

I was walking up to the duplex, about five minutes later, when Canaan's bike turned onto our street. I stopped in the driveway and waved my arms over my head. He didn't notice me, though. Or if he did, he sure didn't act like it. He hopped off his bike and rolled it over to his side of the house. I ran to meet him.

"Hey," I said. "Where you been? Ain't seen you much."

"Busy," he muttered. He turned around and walked past me, back to the front of the house. I followed.

"Well, I've got good news! Mr. Briggs has a job for

us. He wants us to deliver some of those little wooden carvings he makes. There's loads of them. And you know how much he likes us, so he'll pay real good I bet."

"Do it yourself," Canaan said. He was halfway up the steps to his front door, reaching for the handle.

"Hey." I reached out and grabbed his arm, but he jerked away. "What's going on? I can't keep doing all this by myself. We're supposed to do this together. Don't you wanna go to the circus this summer?"

"I don't really care."

"You used to. . . . What's going on? What's wrong?"

He turned around so fast that I stumbled backwards. He looked so mad. So mean. "Don't you get it? He ain't coming back, Nola! He left us. He left and he didn't say good-bye and he ain't coming back."

I shook my head. "No, he will. He couldn't have left for good. Your daddy wouldn't do that."

"Well then, where is he?" Canaan yelled. He'd never yelled at me before. "Why ain't he back yet? Brian's right. He's gone."

"Canaan . . ." I started to reach for his hand, but he shoved both of them into his pockets and stepped back. "I'm sorry. I —"

"You're lucky your dad's dead," he snapped.

It took a minute to realize what he'd just said. My face got hot all of a sudden, and it wasn't from the summer heat, neither. I wanted to hit him. Punch him right in the mouth. Or kick him, maybe. But I'd never been in a fight before. Especially not with a boy. Especially not with Canaan. So I just stood there for a second with my mouth open.

I expected him to apologize right away. To say something like "Nola, I didn't mean that" and to reach for my arm, then it would be my turn to jerk away. Then I'd run off and he'd chase after me, feeling horrible for what he'd said and desperately needing my forgiveness. Just like boys always did in TV shows and in movies.

That's not what happened, though.

Canaan didn't say another word. He just turned around, walked inside his house, and slammed the door in my face.

I told myself not to cry, but by the time I opened my front door, my face was already soaked with angry tears.

# Six Summers Ago

"Mama, can I go play with the boys?" I asked one cloudy Sunday in June. Mama was mopping the kitchen floor while I sat at the table scribbling in a Disney Princess coloring book. She looked over her shoulder at me and shook her head.

"Not today, Nola Baby."

"How come?"

"It's Father's Day. I'm sure they're doing something with their daddy today."

"Oh." I looked down at my box of crayons. I hated Father's Day — all the TV commercials talked about it for weeks, and it made me sad. It's not that I missed my daddy — I didn't remember him, so I couldn't miss him — but I felt left out. Like it was a club I wasn't allowed to be part of. This whole special day everybody but me got to enjoy.

Maybe Mama could tell I was upset because then she said, "Hey, I have an idea. Later on today, why don't we go out to eat? We can head into town, get dinner somewhere nice, and eat ice cream after? What do you think?"

I was about to answer when somebody knocked on the front door. Mama leaned the mop against the counter, wiped her hands on her jeans, and walked into the living room.

I kept coloring until I heard her say, "Oh. Hi, Canaan."

"Hi, Mrs. Sutton. Is Nola here?"

"Yes she is."

I hopped out of my chair and ran to stand next to Mama at the front door. "Hey, Canaan."

He grinned at me. He was missing two of his front teeth — one on the bottom, one on the top. "Wanna come over? We're having hot dogs and there's a cake and stuff."

I looked up at Mama. "Can I?"

"Well . . . Are your parents all right with it, Canaan?"

He nodded.

"Well then, I guess it's fine. Be back by dark, okay?"

"I will! Bye, Mama." I was already out the door, running down the front steps and across the patch of grass between our driveways with Canaan at my side. "I wanted to come over earlier," I told him before we reached his front steps. "But Mama said it was Father's Day and y'all would be doing something."

"That's why we have a cake," he told me. "But I told Mama it wasn't fair that you didn't get cake just because you don't got a dad. I asked if we could pretend my dad was your dad for today, and she said that we could."

*I smiled. It wasn't about the cake or about Mr. Swift being my pretend daddy for a day — I was just glad not to be left out and even gladder that Canaan had included me without me having to ask. We were only six, but he already knew me better than anyone ever could. He knew how I thought and felt and he wouldn't let me be alone. I couldn't have asked for a better best friend. Or a better Father's Day.*

# Chapter Five

I was officially not speaking to Canaan Swift. I planned to tell him so the next day, but he wasn't outside when I left to get the delivery list from Mr. Briggs or when I came back that evening. And I certainly wasn't gonna knock on his door after the way he'd talked to me yesterday.

"At least that means you don't gotta do as much work," Felicia said a couple days later. I had to walk Mrs. Santos's pit bull, Lulu, and I'd asked Felicia if she wanted to take JW for a walk at the same time.

"What do you mean?" I asked. I was a little out of breath. Lulu was strong, and I almost had to jog to keep her from dragging me along behind her.

"Well, if you're not talking to Canaan, that means y'all aren't going to the circus, right?" she asked. "So you don't gotta save all that money."

"We're still gonna go," I said.

"You are?"

I nodded. "We've been planning this for a long time — not just me and Canaan, but all three of the boys. We have to go, and I've gotta save up the money."

"Doesn't seem fair," Felicia said. "You saving up all the money by yourself for their circus tickets. I wouldn't do it. Especially if he said something that ugly to me."

"Canaan's my best friend," I said. "I know he didn't mean it. In a couple weeks he'll come around begging for forgiveness, and I'm not gonna let a couple weeks of fighting ruin our plans. Besides, it's not just about him. Kevin and Brian are coming, too. And Kevin's too little to remember the last circus, so he *has* to go this year."

"Well, even if you're still mad at him, I hope you'll come to my birthday party this weekend."

"Of course," I said. "No way I'd miss it."

We stopped on the corner so Lulu could pee on Miss Shirley's plants. Then JW squatted down in the grass beside the hydrangeas.

"Ewwww," Felicia said, looking away. "You think Miss Shirley'd be mad if I didn't scoop after JW? She's always so nice. . . ."

"Yeah, she's nice, but you still oughta clean up after him. She can't see real well. She might step in it."

Felicia sighed and pulled a plastic baggie out of her back pocket. "Ugh. I know I wanted a dog, and I love JW and all, but I am not sure it's worth it."

\* \* \*

On Saturday morning, I delivered the last two wooden carvings for Mr. Briggs. Even though he didn't want money, almost every person I took them to wanted to give Mr. Briggs something. It was rare I left one of the houses on his list without a Tupperware container full of cookies or a jar of frozen strawberry preserves.

No wonder he was all right paying us. He probably saved a bunch of money on groceries.

"Thank you very much, Nola," Mr. Briggs said when I came by to hand over today's gifts. "I appreciate your help this week."

"You're welcome, Mr. Briggs," I said.

"Now, where's Canaan?" he asked as he reached into his pocket and removed a battered brown wallet. "I thought he was helping you."

"It's a long story," I told him. "But I don't mind doing it on my own."

"Well, I hope everything's all right," he said. "I haven't seen the boys outside too much lately."

I wasn't sure what to say to that.

"Here you are," he said, handing me two crisp ten-dollar bills.

"Oh, Mr. Briggs, I can't take this much —"

"Yes you can," he said. "And you will. That's also payment for one last delivery, if you don't mind."

"Sure. What is it?"

"Just one second," he said.

But it took him about thirty to get to his feet. He sighed and groaned and put a hand on his lower back as he straightened up. Then he walked across the porch and opened the screen door of his house. He was gone inside for a few minutes, and I waited on the steps, watching a couple hummingbirds swarm around the feeder in Mrs. Santos's garden across the street.

When Mr. Briggs came back outside, he was clutching one of his small wooden statues in his thin, dark hands. "Today is Felicia Hooper's birthday," he said. "I believe she's having a party?"

"Yes, sir," I said. "This afternoon at three. I'm going."

"I thought you might be, which is why I'm hoping you won't mind giving this to her." He handed me the little carving. It was a girl with long braids holding a small puppy in her arms. It was the most detailed of his trinkets I'd seen, and I knew it must have taken forever to whittle.

I also knew the girl was Felicia.

"This is beautiful," I told him.

He gave me a big smile, then eased himself back down onto the top step. "Y'all kids make me smile every day. I thought I ought to return the favor. Tell her I said happy birthday."

"I sure will. Thanks again, Mr. Briggs."

"Have a nice afternoon, Nola."

I went home and changed into a pair of clean denim shorts and my favorite purple T-shirt. Mama helped me straighten my hair while Richard wrapped Felicia's present — a copy of *The Giver*, a book I'd read in my English class and knew she'd like. I always gave Felicia books. She read more than anyone I knew, even in the summer when she didn't have to.

"You're making a mess of that." Mama laughed. "Have you ever wrapped a present before?"

"Honestly? No," Richard said. "I always buy gift bags."

"Men," Mama snorted. She ran the straightener through my hair one more time, then said, "All done. Go put your shoes on and I'll rewrap Felicia's gift."

"It doesn't look that bad, does it?" Richard asked.

"Uh . . ." I chewed on my bottom lip. "Well . . ."

"Nola doesn't want to be rude, but yes, sweetheart. It looks terrible." Mama kissed him on the cheek. "That's okay. We all have our faults."

I put on my tennis shoes and waited for Mama to finish rewrapping the present. "Have fun, Nola Baby," she said, hugging me before I headed out the door. "Be home before dark."

"I will, Mama."

There were a lot of kids at Felicia's party — people from her class, from her church, all her cousins, and then us kids from the subdivision. There weren't even enough folding chairs in her backyard for everyone to sit in. It was the biggest birthday party I'd ever been to.

Not everyone was there, though.

"I thought you invited the Swift boys?" I asked Felicia while Mrs. Hooper cut into the cake. We'd just sang "Happy Birthday" and, with everyone gathered around, it was obvious I hadn't just overlooked them. Canaan, Kevin, and Brian were nowhere to be seen.

"I did," she said. "I guess they didn't want to come."

She looked kinda sad about that, and I understood why. Felicia had never been as close to the boys as me, but she'd known them all her life, too. She'd been to all our birthday parties and built snow forts with us in the winter and invited us over for snacks after school. It was weird for the boys not to come to her party, and it must have hurt her feelings.

Mrs. Hooper handed her a huge piece of lemon birthday cake and everyone else started lining up, ready to get some for themselves. I got the second piece, after Felicia, then sat down in a chair to eat. Usually, I sat with Canaan and the other Swift boys at parties and cookouts. But without them around, I found myself sitting alone.

Now I was the one feeling a little sad.

But then JW ran over to me, panting and wagging his little puppy tail. He jumped up to put his front paws on my knee and looked up at me. Like he could sense that I was down and wanted to cheer me up. Or like he saw the cake in my hand and wanted a bite. I didn't mind either way.

"He's a cute dog."

I looked over and saw Teddy Ryan walking toward the empty chair beside mine, carrying a very, very small slice of cake on a blue paper plate.

"Yeah," I said. "He is."

Teddy sat down in the folding chair beside me. He wiggled around for a second, trying to get comfortable, then he pushed his glasses up his nose. He was wearing a striped shirt and khakis — he *always* wore khakis. Never blue jeans. His hair was real neat, cut close to his head. He looked too dressed up for a backyard birthday party, all crisp and clean except for a couple of red bumps speckling his dark skin, right along his chin and nose.

Pimples. A lot of the kids in my class had them now, and Mama said I'd have to deal with them soon enough.

I knew it was rude to stare, but Teddy had been so mean to me that I figured it was at least sort of all right. I would have stared even if those pimples weren't gross. I was shocked he was sitting next to me. And nervous. Last time he was this close to me, I ended up with gum in my hair.

"So what did you get Felicia?" he asked, poking at his tiny slice of cake with a plastic fork.

JW got tired of waiting on me to give him cake, so he left me and wandered over to a group of girls from Felicia's church, walking around them in circles while he waited for scraps to fall. In my head, I was begging him to come back. Then I could pretend I was too distracted by the dog to talk to Teddy Ryan.

"Just a book."

"Oh, which book?"

If Canaan were here, he'd say, "None of your business," and ignore Teddy until he went away. But I couldn't be *that* rude, even when I wanted to.

"*The Giver.*"

"I like that book. I got it for Christmas from my uncle Clayton."

I nodded. Neither of us said anything for a few minutes, and even though I didn't like Teddy at all, I didn't like being so quiet, either. So I looked over at him and his empty plate and asked, "Why did you get such a small piece of cake?"

He looked embarrassed. "Don't tell my mom I ate it. I'm not supposed to have any at all."

"Why not?"

"I have a lot of allergies."

"You're allergic to cake?" I asked. I couldn't imagine anything worse.

"Not to cake. To the stuff in cake. It makes me throw up."

"Ew. So why'd you eat it?"

"Because it tastes good."

I laughed, and he smiled at me. He had huge front teeth. Twice the size of the others in his mouth. It was an awful funny smile, and that made me laugh even more. Which made him laugh, too.

"Where's Canaan?" he asked once we'd both stopped giggling.

I shrugged. "I'm not speaking to him."

"Yeah. Me neither."

"What reason do you got for not speaking to him?"

"He's always been mean to me."

"He's mean to you because you're mean to me," I told him.

"I'm not mean to you."

I almost laughed. "You are so. You're always kicking my seat on the bus or pulling on my ponytail. And you stuck gum in my hair. Mama had to chop it all off, and I was trying to grow it long. That's mean."

Teddy looked down at his empty plate. He looked embarrassed, but I had no idea what for. "I wasn't trying to be mean."

"Well, you were. You're the mean one," I told him. "Canaan's really nice, actually."

"Then how come you're not talking to him?" Teddy asked.

I chewed on my bottom lip. "Because . . . he's being mean to me now, too."

Teddy opened his mouth to say something, but Felicia hollered for me before he could get the words out. I was glad for a reason to get away from him and the questions about Canaan.

"Come over here," Felicia said, grabbing my arm and dragging me over to the present table. "I can tell your present's a book — I wanna open it first."

I glanced back at Teddy once. He just sat there, holding his empty plate and looking as lonely as I'd felt a few minutes ago.

A couple hours later, the party was over and everyone started heading home. Somehow, I ended up with Teddy Ryan again, just outside the Hoopers' house. We had to cross the same street, and we walked together, not saying a word until we got to the side we lived on.

"Your hair looks real pretty like that," Teddy said out of the blue. "I'm sorry I put gum in it last year. . . . Anyway, bye."

Then he took off like a lightning bolt toward his house.

I just stood on the sidewalk, staring after him. I wasn't sure what to make of that, but I decided it was nice of him to apologize.

Too bad Teddy Ryan wasn't the boy I wanted an apology from.

# Last Summer

*Our town has a fair every August, just a few days before school
starts. It's not real big — just a few rides and some games and
lots of tables selling barbecue that Mama says is the best in the
world. We looked forward to it every year, though, especially
now that we were old enough that our parents let us walk
around by ourselves.*

*We rode the Scrambler and the Ferris wheel over and over
until Kevin said he was sick to his stomach, then the four of us
headed across the lawn to the stage where a local band was
playing country music.*

*"Can we go watch the tractor pull?" Kevin asked. "Please,
please, please? I love tractors. Especially them big ones with
big wheels. I want one, but our backyard is too small. Can we
go see the tractor pull, please?"*

*"I thought we were gonna listen to the music," I said.*

*"I don't like this song," Kevin whined.*

*"But Nola does," Canaan said. He was right. The band
was playing my favorite Miranda Lambert song, and the girl
singing was doing a real good job. I wasn't surprised at all that
he remembered I liked it without me having to tell him, but it
still made me smile.*

Kevin started to pout. "Okay . . . But I really, really want to see the tractors."

"We don't have to stay," I said. I didn't want Kevin to miss out on what he wanted to do because of me. I'd feel real awful if he was upset.

"But you hate the tractor pull," Canaan said. "You always fall asleep when we watch it." He turned to Kevin. "And we're older, so what we say goes."

"I'll take him," Brian said.

Kevin's face lit up. "You will?"

"I don't like country music much, anyway. I can go with him if y'all will be okay on your own?"

"We're not babies, Brian," Canaan said. "We'll be fine."

So Kevin and Brian left and it was just me and Canaan and the loud music and a cool, soft patch of grass to sit on. We sang along to the songs for a while and sometimes Canaan would change the words, making up silly new versions to make me laugh. We'd sat through about three songs when I heard someone hollering to me.

"Nola! Hey, Nola!"

Canaan glanced over his shoulder and groaned. "Uh-oh."

"What? Who is it?" I turned and saw Teddy Ryan walking toward us, holding a can of Coke and dressed in a barbecue-stained striped shirt and khakis. My heart sank. Today was going so well — I didn't want Teddy Ryan to ruin it.

"Hi, Nola," he said when he reached us.

"Um . . . hi."

"What are y'all doing?"

"None of your business," Canaan said. He stood up and held out a hand to me. "Come on, Nola. Let's go somewhere else."

I stood up and let him pull me away. Teddy hollered to me again. "Nola, wait up. I brought this for you." But Canaan kept pulling me along, so I kept my head down and pretended not to hear him, which was rude of me, but it was Teddy Ryan and he was always picking on me, so he deserved it. Whatever he'd brought for me, I knew it wasn't good.

We'd only taken a few steps when I suddenly felt something cold and wet splash all over my back and legs. I stopped, startled, and it took me a minute to realize what had happened. Teddy had just thrown the Coke all over me.

"What'd you do that for?" Canaan yelled. Teddy didn't get a chance to answer before Canaan was pulling me along behind him again, telling Teddy over his shoulder, "Leave her alone. I mean it."

Canaan helped me find a water fountain and I did my best to wash off all the sticky spots the Coke had left on my arms and legs, but there was no saving my shirt. It was white and now it was stained with a big brownish-yellow splotch.

"This is one of my favorite shirts," I said, trying not to cry. It was a stupid thing to cry about, but I couldn't help it.

"I bet it'll wash out." Canaan reached out and squeezed my hand. "He's a jerk. Don't let him get to you. He ain't worth crying over."

We spent the rest of the night playing the fair games, and Canaan won me a stuffed moose and, despite Teddy Ryan's best efforts, it was still one of the most wonderful nights of the summer.

# Chapter
# Six

The smell of bacon woke me up the next morning. Richard was in the kitchen, standing in front of the stove, when I came out of my room.

"Good morning, kiddo," he said. "Breakfast will be ready in a few minutes."

"Where's Mama?" I asked.

"Your grandmother called and wanted her help with something. I told her I'd come over and make you breakfast."

I folded my arms over my chest. "Why would you need to make me breakfast? Usually if Mama's gone I just make myself some cereal or pop a frozen waffle in the toaster."

"All right, you caught me." He put some bacon on a plate with a couple pieces of toast and handed it to me. "I'm procrastinating."

I smiled. "Procrastinating" had been one of my vocabulary words in English class last year. Richard had helped me with that list. When I asked him what "procrastinating" meant, he'd said:

"It means to put something off as long as you can. Like right now — you're asking me about your vocabulary list even though your test isn't until Friday. Because you're *procrastinating* cleaning your room like your mother told you to an hour ago."

Richard loved my vocabulary lists. Every time I brought one home, he wanted to read the words and look them all up in the dictionary, even if he knew what they meant. He said I oughta know the exact definition. Then he'd use them all in regular conversation so that I got used to hearing them. I wasn't even in school anymore and he was still using my vocab words when he talked to me.

I started chewing on a piece of bacon. "What are you procrastinating?" I asked.

"I promised to clean up the yard — you know, mow

the grass, pull the weeds, water the plants. All that good stuff." He made himself a plate and sat at the little dining table. I sat down across from him. "I shouldn't be complaining to you, though. You've been working your behind off, haven't you?"

My mouth was full of toast, so I just nodded.

"What kind of jobs do you have lined up today?" he asked.

I swallowed and wiped my mouth with the back of my hand. "Nothing. I was gonna walk Lulu, but Mrs. Santos decided to go down to Tennessee to visit her sister, and she took the dog with her."

"Well," Richard said, "if you're free today, I might have a job for you."

"You want me to do the yard?"

"Not all of it," he said. "But if you wanted to, I'd pay you to help me. Canaan, too, if he wants to join you."

I looked down at my plate. "It'll just be me."

Richard didn't say anything for a minute. I was just glad he didn't ask me why Canaan and the other boys hadn't been coming around. I'd been getting that question from everybody lately, and I never did know how to answer it.

"Tell you what," Richard said. "Why don't we split the work? I take care of mowing if you'll pull the weeds and pick up all the sticks."

"And you'll pay me?"

"Of course."

I narrowed my eyes. "You know my rates, don't you? I don't work for cheap."

He laughed. "I figured. I'd say there's about an hour of work out there. I'll give you ten bucks for it."

I nodded. "Fair enough." And we shook on it.

After I got dressed, I headed outside to get started. It was the most humid day we'd had all summer. My hair puffed up right away, and I could already feel sweat collecting on my neck and under my bangs. Five steps out the door, and I was already wondering if the ten dollars was worth it.

I headed to the backyard first, since that's where most of the twigs and sticks were. At first I didn't even notice him sitting there. Not until I heard a sniff. A loud one. The kinda sniff you only hear from someone who's got a bad cold or who's been crying. That's when I looked over and saw him, sitting on the ground next to the swing set, picking at the grass with his fingertips.

"Brian?"

He didn't look up, so I couldn't see his face. But his voice was cracked and wet when he said, "Hey, Nola."

His hair was dirty. Oily and tangled like he hadn't bothered to wash or brush it in days. There was a red stain near the collar of his white T-shirt. He looked a real mess.

I sat down in the grass, facing him. "What's wrong?"

"Nothing."

"Where are your brothers?"

"Inside."

"Brian." I reached out and put my hand over his so he'd stop picking at the grass. There were dozens of broken blades on his bare knees. "Come on. You can talk to me."

"Talking won't help anything," he said.

"Is it about your daddy?" I asked. "I know he's not back yet. I'm real sorry, Brian."

"Screw him," Brian snarled.

It made me nervous, hearing Brian talk like that. He was always so calm and quiet. The quietest of the Swift brothers, hands down. He was the one who broke up the fights. I'd seen him tired, I'd seen him annoyed, I'd seen him sad. But I'd never seen Brian angry.

And even now, it didn't last long. He sighed and sniffed again, and just like that, the anger had switched back to sadness.

"What can I do to help?" I asked. "Just tell me. I'll help with anything I can."

"I can't . . . I can't do this," he said. Finally, he looked up at me. His glasses were tilted to the side a little, and his face was all puffy and red. "I can't keep doing everything."

"What do you mean?"

"It was bad enough when they fought all the time, but now Dad's gone and all Mama does is sleep and cry and I gotta do everything," he said. "I do the grocery shopping and the cleaning and the cooking — and I don't even know how to do all that stuff, really. It's too much. I can't keep it up. I can't . . ." His words were swallowed up by sudden, gasping sobs.

I'd never seen a boy his age cry. Boys Kevin's age, sure, but not teenage boys. And especially not like this, where he was crying so hard I thought he might choke or throw up. I squeezed his hand, but I didn't bother saying a word. He wouldn't have been able to hear me over his own gasps.

He quieted a couple minutes later, but there were still tears running down his face.

"I can help," I said. "I can cook a couple things — mostly things in the microwave — and Mama taught me how to make an omelet a few weeks ago. And I'm not terrible at cleaning."

He let out a long breath. "Thanks," he said. "But I think I just . . . I need to get out of here for a while."

His hand slipped out from under mine when he stood up. I stood up, too. "Where you going?"

"I don't know. To a friend's house or something. I just need a break."

I followed him to the side of the duplex, where the boys' bikes were. His was the biggest. Black and blue and with handle brakes. He dusted off the seat and started to roll the bike around to the front yard.

"Brian," I called after him. He looked back. "If you need anything, I'm right next door. Same goes for the other boys. Me and Canaan ain't speaking right now, but I'd still help him if he needed me to."

"Thanks, Nola," he said.

I didn't watch him ride away. I didn't like watching the boys leave while I was still standing there. It seemed to be happening too much lately. So instead I headed to the backyard before he could pedal away.

Richard's guess was about right. I spent an hour pulling weeds and getting the yard ready for him to mow — putting away all the things we'd left in the yard, like Mrs. Swift's lawn chair. It had been out there since the last day of school. The day Mr. Swift left. It was dirty and still wet from a summer storm a few nights earlier. I folded it up and leaned it against their side of the duplex, right next to the bikes.

I thought about Brian all day. About the horrible, hurting sounds he made when he cried. Like everything inside of him hurt so bad he couldn't even breathe. I tried to think of ways I could help him. Of ways I could get Mama to help without the boys taking it as charity.

That was the real tricky thing. There were a lot of people bad off where we lived. Most people didn't make too much money. But you couldn't just hand them the things they needed, especially if they didn't ask you to. Mama said that made people feel ashamed. It hurt their pride to take charity. I never really understood it. I thought everything would be easier if people just said what they needed and let others help if they could.

I didn't want to make the boys feel worse, though. It was one thing for me to offer to make them omelets. It was another to get Mama to do their laundry or help buy their groceries. Not that she could afford that, either.

Later that evening, while Mama was cooking dinner, I sat in my room with a pad of colored construction paper in my lap and a pack of markers next to me. I was making a birthday card for Richard, who was turning thirty-five in a few days. Normally I would have just gotten a card from the rack at the drugstore, but Mama said Richard liked my homemade cards better. She said they meant more. I didn't mind making one. I liked to draw, so it was kinda fun.

I'd just finished writing Richard's name in bubble letters on a piece of green paper when I noticed something out the window. I looked up and stared through the glass, out into the backyard. Kevin was sitting on the swings, pushing himself back and forth with one foot on the ground. He was alone, and I wondered if Brian had gotten home yet.

"Nola!" Mama called from the kitchen. "Dinner's ready."

"Coming." I put my art supplies aside and slid off my bed. I'd already decided what I was gonna do before I even got to the kitchen. "Just a second," I told Mama. "I'll be right back."

"All right. Well, hurry it up before your food gets cold."

I walked out the front door and headed around to the backyard. I took a deep breath and put a big old smile on my face. "Kevin!" I hollered in a happy, cheerful voice. "Hey, I was hoping to find you out here."

He looked up, but he didn't say nothing. I wondered if that meant he still wasn't speaking at all.

"Mama made way too much for dinner," I said. It was only a little lie. Mama always made a little too much for dinner. Just maybe not *way* too much. "You wanna come over and eat with us? We ain't got room in the fridge for any more leftovers."

He hesitated a second, but then he slid off his swing and walked over to me. He still didn't say anything. Not a word. Not a sound.

"All right," I said. "Come on."

Kevin ate with us that night, but no matter how much Mama and I talked to him, he kept silent. He'd shake his head or nod, but that was it. And most of the time, he just looked sad. His big eyes drooped, and he was almost always looking down. It broke my heart. And I could see it was breaking Mama's, too, though she didn't say a word about Mr. or Mrs. Swift.

After dinner, Kevin helped me wash the dishes. Then we watched TV together right up until Mama said he oughta get home because it was close to bedtime. I watched him walk back to his side of the duplex through the living room window. At a distance, it looked like Kevin, the little boy I'd grown up with, and for a second, I could pretend nothing had changed.

But it had.

It all changed that night I saw Mr. Swift pull out of the driveway. And the only way everything would go back to normal was if Mr. Swift came back.

Just then, I knew what I had to do.

# Three Summers Ago

*It was raining the day Mama told me she wanted me to meet Richard. She said it like it was no big deal while she was getting ready for work one morning. "Oh, Nola Baby, that man I've been seeing — Richard — he's coming over for dinner tonight. He's excited to meet you."*

*I smiled because that was what I was supposed to do — because that was the polite thing. And I said I was looking forward to meeting him. I said he sounded real nice. I said fried chicken and mashed potatoes sounded great for dinner.*

*But the minute Mama's car was out of the driveway and down the road, I ran over to the Swifts' house, still wearing my purple pajamas and a pair of old flip-flops that were a size or two too small. There was a good summer storm going, and by the time Brian answered the door, I was soaked and shaking.*

*"Is Canaan here?"*

*Brian shook his head as he stepped aside to let me in. "He and Kevin are at the doctor."*

*"Are they all right?"*

*"Yeah. Just getting a checkup. Why are you in your pajamas? And why don't you have an umbrella?"*

*I kicked off my flip-flops so I wouldn't get the carpet all* wet, but my hair and clothes were still dripping, so it didn't do much good. "I wanted to talk to Canaan real bad, so I just ran out of the house. How long do you think he'll be gone?"

"They just left, so probably quite a while."

"Oh." I wrapped my arms around myself and looked down at my feet, feeling silly and sad all at once.

"You can talk to me, though, if you want. I don't mind."

"Really?"

Brian was eleven then, and he seemed so much older than Canaan and me. He never minded if we tagged along, but I always wondered if I was bothering him. I wondered that about almost everybody, though. Except Canaan, of course.

"Sure. Come on in. I'll get you a towel."

I dried off a little, then I spread the towel out on the couch so I wouldn't get the cushion wet when I sat down. "Mama wants me to meet her boyfriend," I told Brian. "His name's Richard and he's coming over for dinner tonight."

"You don't seem too happy about it."

"I'm nervous. What do I say to him? What if he doesn't like me?"

"Why wouldn't he like you?" Brian asked.

"I . . . I don't know. I don't know how to act around him. I don't know anybody else whose mamas have boyfriends.

They all just have daddies, and I've never had one of them, neither. I don't know what to do. What am I supposed to do?"

I didn't realize I'd started to cry until Brian reached out and touched my arm. "It's okay. Calm down. You don't gotta do anything."

"Why does she have to have a boyfriend, anyway? I like things the way they are — just her and me."

"She's not going nowhere, Nola," he said. "Even if she's got a boyfriend, she's still gonna be around."

"I don't know. I don't like it."

"You don't gotta like it," he said. "But you know, you ain't met him yet. You might like him. And I know he'll like you. Everybody does. Maybe don't think about it like losing your mom — look at it like getting a new person. Ain't it better to have two people who love you than one?"

"Well, I guess so."

"It'll be okay," he said, giving me a hug even though I was still wet from the rain. "I promise."

That was the day I realized just how smart Brian was. He always knew the right thing to say. He always thought about things I didn't. I thought he could solve every problem. I thought he could make everything better.

I thought Brian had all the answers.

# Chapter Seven

When Canaan and I were in fifth grade, we were obsessed with detective and spy movies. We liked to try and solve crimes around the subdivision. Like who stole Mrs. Hooper's garden gnome or who wasn't scooping after their dog and leaving poop on the sidewalk. We were pretty good at it, too. We never solved any mysteries or anything, but we found out a lot of stuff about people, that was for sure.

And if I'd learned anything from all that detective work, it was that Edna, the manager at Rocky's, was the person to talk to when you needed to know anything about anybody. She knew it all.

So late Monday afternoon I rode my bike up to Rocky's, hoping I might find out something about where Mr. Swift had gone.

"Nola!" Edna exclaimed when I walked through the door, bells jingling overhead. "Long time no see. Where you been, sweetheart?"

"Working, mostly," I said. "Trying to save up some money."

"Well, I've sure missed you in here. And the boys. Where's Canaan? I don't know if I've ever seen you come in here without him."

"They're, uh, they're at home," I said.

Edna nodded knowingly. "I hear they're going through a tough time. My prayers are with them. But I'm glad you came in. What can I get you today?"

I ordered an orange milkshake and waited by the counter, chatting with Edna while she made it for me. It wasn't too busy, so she didn't mind talking to me. I told her all about my different jobs and Felicia's birthday party. I just jabbered on while I tried to think of a way to ask her what I really wanted to.

Luckily, she brought it up on her own.

"So how are the boys doing with all this?" she asked in a low, secret voice. "Really."

I took a long slurp on my straw before answering. "Not too good," I said. "They're real upset about their daddy."

"Bless their hearts," Edna said. "And their poor mama, too."

"I know." I took a deep breath, knowing this was my chance to ask the question. The whole reason I'd come here. "Where do you think Mr. Swift might have gone?"

"Who knows?" Edna said. "Although, I did see his car in Bunker the other day when I went to Walmart. At least it looked like his car."

"Really? Just over in Bunker?" I asked.

"Mmhm. Out on the highway. No idea where he was headed to, but I could've sworn it was him."

"If he's just over in Bunker, why hasn't he come to see the boys?" I didn't even mean to ask it out loud. It was just the first question that came to mind. Somehow, I figured Mr. Swift had gone somewhere far away. Like Siberia. Or Tennessee. Not Bunker, a city about fifteen minutes away.

Edna didn't answer. She picked up a rag and started wiping off the counter. But there was something dark in her eyes. Either sad or mad, I don't know. But it made her look even more like a ghost than usual.

Not long after, customers started heading into Rocky's, picking up dinner on their way home from work. I said good-bye to Edna and rode my bike back home. As soon as I got inside, I went straight for the phone.

I'd just punched in a few numbers when the front door opened and Mama came in with a couple bags of groceries. "Hey, Nola Baby," she said. "How was your day?"

"Fine," I said, pressing the phone to my ear as it started to ring.

"Who are you calling?" Mama asked.

"Grandma Lucy."

Mama's face scrunched up, and I knew she was thinking, *Why on earth would you do that?* I didn't have time to answer, though, because Grandma Lucy had already picked up the phone on her end.

"Hello? Who is it?"

My stomach rumbled, the way it always did when I talked to Grandma Lucy. She was the crankiest person

I'd ever met. And the loudest. She yelled all day long, and at everybody.

"Hi, Grandma Lucy," I said. "It's me. . . . It's Nola."

"What do you want? I can't talk long. I'm about to sit down to eat."

"Oh, okay. I just wanted to know if you had any, uh, work I could do for you? Like help with your garden or cleaning the house? Something I could help with?"

"Work?" Grandma Lucy asked. "What are you looking for work for?"

"I'm trying to save up some money," I told her. "For the circus."

"So you want me to pay you?" she asked.

"Um, yeah. If you want . . . I wasn't trying to be rude or nothing. I'm sorry."

She sighed. "The garage needs to be cleaned out. You can come help with that this weekend. I'm sure I can give you a little money."

"Okay. Thank you, Grandma Lucy. I appreciate it."

"All right. Good-bye, then."

"Bye."

Mama was in the kitchen putting groceries away when I hung up the phone. She looked over at me, one eyebrow raised. "You must really be desperate for work," she said, "if you're willing to ask your grandmother."

I shrugged. The truth was, I hated asking Grandma Lucy for a job. Mostly because it meant I'd have to spend an afternoon with her. But I had a reason. She lived in Bunker, and that meant I might get a chance to hunt down Mr. Swift. Spending time with Grandma Lucy was a price I was willing to pay to get the boys back to the way they were.

"Where's Richard?" I asked Mama.

"He said he was busy tonight," she said. "But he wants to take me out tomorrow night. To a nice restaurant. I don't know what the occasion is, though. I keep worrying I'm forgetting our anniversary or something. But that's not for a few weeks yet."

"That sounds fun," I said. "Are you gonna wear a dress and everything?"

"I suppose so. Maybe my blue one . . . Hmmm." She finished with the groceries, then turned to look at me. "By the way, I know you're too old for a babysitter, but since I'm going to be out late tomorrow night, I asked Mrs. Hooper from across the street to come check in on you."

"Okay," I said.

"Actually," Mama continued, "I asked her to start checking in on you during the day, too. I know Mrs. Swift usually does that, but with everything going on . . ." She trailed off, sighed, and finished with, "Well, she's got a lot going on. And I'd feel better if Mrs. Hooper looked after you a little."

For some reason, I immediately wanted to defend Mrs. Swift, even though Mama hadn't said nothing bad about her. But the truth was, Mrs. Swift hadn't checked on me at all over the past couple weeks. I hadn't even seen her since that last day of school when she was drinking sweet tea in her lawn chair. Pretty much anybody in the subdivision could tell you where I'd been. Someone was always looking after me while I was working for them. But not Mrs. Swift.

So I just nodded and said, "All right."

Mama stretched out her arm and ran a hand through my messy hair. Then she turned toward the kitchen, staring at the cabinets full of groceries. "This is pathetic," she said, "but I don't feel like cooking. Pizza?"

"Sounds good to me," I said.

* * *

I was already in bed when Mama got home from her date with Richard the next night, but I hadn't quite fallen asleep yet. I heard the key turn in the lock, followed by a bunch of laughing and whispering. And I thought I heard Mama singing, too. Something was definitely up.

And I found out what the next night, when Mama and Richard sat me down on the couch after dinner.

"We need to talk to you about something, kiddo," Richard said.

"Something good," Mama said quickly. "You're not in trouble or anything, baby. I know you're a worrier, but this is something good. Real good."

Richard nodded. "Very good. Superb, even."

I laughed. "Superb" was another one of my vocabulary words from last year.

"Well," Mama said. "Something happened last night. Richard and I made a decision, and, well . . ." She lifted up her left hand, pressing her fingers to her mouth. And that's when I saw the ring. A tiny little diamond on a gold band. I'd seen enough TV to know what that meant.

"Y'all are getting married?" I asked. I could feel the grin splitting my face as the words tumbled out.

Mama nodded, hand still over her mouth. But I could tell by the way her eyes scrunched up that she was grinning, too.

"You okay with that, kiddo?" Richard asked.

"Yeah," I said. "It's about time!"

They both laughed. Mama wrapped her arms around me, pressing her face into my hair. "I'm so happy, Nola Baby," she whispered. Then she kissed my cheek and pulled away.

"There's more," Richard said. "The wedding will be at the end of the summer, right before you go back to school. And then —"

"And then we're moving!" Mama exclaimed. She threw her hands over her head when she said it, like she had just told me we were going to Disney World. Like she expected me to scream and jump up and down when I heard the news.

I didn't.

My heart sank into my stomach and I felt the grin slip right off my mouth. "What?" I asked.

"Not far," Richard said quickly. "You'd still go to the same middle school."

"But . . . we'd be leaving the duplex?"

"Of course," Mama said. "Nola Baby, this place is hardly big enough for me and you. It's way too small for all three of us."

"Where would we be going?" I asked.

"Just across town, probably," she said. "Not that far."

But it was far. Across town was too far to ride my bike to Rocky's. Across town was too far to walk to Felicia's house or Mr. Briggs's front porch or Teddy Ryan's trampoline.

Across town was too far from the Swift boys.

"I don't wanna go," I said.

"What's wrong, kiddo?" Richard asked.

"I don't wanna go," I repeated, feeling like a baby but unable to help myself. "Can't we just . . . can't we just stay here?"

"Nola," Mama said. "We can't live in this little duplex forever."

But we were supposed to. I was *always* supposed to live next door to Canaan and Brian and Kevin. Always. How could I ever live all the way across town? How could I be that far away from them?

I felt tears burning my eyes.

"Oh, baby." Mama reached out to hug me, but I

jumped off the couch, ducking under her arms, and took off for my room. I was mad at her. And at Richard. I wanted to yell and stomp my feet and throw things — but I didn't want to get in trouble, so instead I just ran. It was bad enough they wanted me to move, but the way they'd treated it, like it was some sort of exciting present, was the worst.

I heard Mama start to come after me, but then Richard said, "Let her go." And I was glad. I didn't want her to comfort me. Not unless she'd change her mind and say we could stay here.

I slammed my door and buried myself under the covers on my bed. Tears were running, hot, down my face. I wiped them off with the corner of my blanket. I could hear movement through the wall. Muffled words and footsteps. I reached out and knocked, using the code me and Canaan had made up years ago.

Maybe this time he'd answer.

Maybe this time he'd know that I really needed him.

I knocked again and again and again. Waiting.

But he never replied.

# Chapter Eight

The next morning I sucked up my pride and walked over to the Swifts' side of the duplex. No matter what was happening between Canaan and me, I knew he'd want to know about Mama's news. And maybe, deep down, I hoped that hearing I was leaving would make him snap out of this mean streak and be my best friend again, while I was still around.

Brian answered the front door. He looked just as bad as the last time I saw him, only this time he wasn't crying. So that was good.

"Hey, Nola," he said. He sounded exhausted. "What's up?"

"Can I come in?" I asked. "I need to talk to y'all. Especially Canaan."

"Sure." He stepped aside so I could walk into the house. "Kevin's asleep in my room, but Canaan's playing video games."

I couldn't help looking at the living room. If Mama was there, she'd say it looked like a tornado had come through. There were pizza boxes and dirty dishes and piles of clothes all over the place. And not to be mean, but it sort of smelled. I'd never say that to any of the boys, though.

"Where's your mama?" I asked.

"She got a new job at the gas station," he said. "She'll be back later."

"So she's doing better?"

Brian just shrugged. "Come on. Let's tell Canaan you're here."

Canaan was sitting on his bedroom floor with a controller in his hand. His hair was dirty and his clothes looked like they'd been worn for a few days. He didn't look up from the TV when we walked in.

"Hey," I said. "I need to talk to you."

"Then talk," he said, still clicking buttons on his controller.

I looked over at Brian, standing in the doorway, then back at Canaan. "Mama and Richard are getting married," I said. "They told me last night."

The old Canaan would've looked up at me and grinned. He would've been happy for Mama. He would've told me to tell her congratulations. Or he would've told her himself the next time he came over for dinner.

Not this Canaan, though. Instead, he just shrugged and said, "So?"

"Canaan," I said, sitting down on the floor beside him. He still didn't look at me. "Canaan, we're moving. At the end of the summer, after the wedding, Mama and Richard and me are moving — probably across town. We won't be neighbors anymore."

He kept playing his game. It was a racing game. His car swerved and weaved all over the road, bumping and scraping the other vehicles. For a second, all I could think was, *I'm sure glad people don't drive like that in real life*. A second later, though, I realized Canaan still hadn't said a word. Realized he wasn't gonna.

"Did you hear me?" I asked. "I'm gonna be moving. I know you're going through a hard time right now, and I know we ain't talked much lately, but this is a big deal. We've always been neighbors. I . . . I kinda thought we always would be."

"That's dumb," he said.

"You didn't used to think so," I mumbled.

We were both quiet for a while. Every second of silence made my heart hurt a little worse. I wanted to curl into a ball. I wanted to cry. I even wanted to scream at him, but I didn't have the nerve. He didn't even care I was leaving. I knew this summer had been off to a bad start, but was he really not gonna miss me? I'd miss him. Even after what he'd said about me being lucky not to have a father — well, I'd still miss him every single day.

I missed him every day already, and I was just next door.

Brian left and headed back into the living room. I didn't move, though. Part of me hoped Canaan would realize how much I was hurting and apologize. I tried not to let myself hope, though. Instead, I just focused on not crying. My stomach ached and my eyes burned. But

I didn't want to start sobbing right then. He'd already said he thought I was dumb. That would make it worse.

I cleared my throat and tried to make my voice sound upbeat and happy. "Well," I said, "at least we have the circus. That'll be right before the wedding, and I've been working a lot, so I think I might even be able to save up enough money for all four of us. It'll be like a going-away party." I laughed. "A going-away party with people riding elephants and walking tightropes. And —"

Canaan threw his controller on the floor and stood up so fast that I jumped. "Stop talking about the stupid circus!" he yelled.

My lip started to tremble the way it always did when somebody yelled at me. "But —"

"Just stop it!" he yelled. "And go home!"

"Canaan." I stood up. "I just —"

"Go!" He pushed me out of the bedroom. Not hard or nothing. He just put his hands on my arms and made me walk backwards. Then he slammed the door in my face.

I stood there, staring at the silver knob while a lump the size of a baseball worked its way up into my throat.

"Sorry," Brian said from somewhere behind me. "He's been like that with everybody lately. Not just you."

That didn't make it better, though. I wasn't everybody. I was his best friend. His best-best friend. I was supposed to be the one person he liked when he was mad at everybody else. That's what he was to me.

"He'll come around eventually," Brian said. But he didn't sound too hopeful.

"Will you tell Kevin for me when he wakes up?" I asked. "About me moving."

"Sure," he said. "Sorry, Nola."

Two "sorrys" didn't make it hurt any less, though. I shook my head and walked out the front door, walking fast so that he wouldn't see the tears starting down my cheeks.

It sure felt like I'd been crying a lot lately.

I don't know why I headed toward Teddy Ryan's backyard. I just didn't want to go home yet, and I saw that his parents' car wasn't in the driveway. The trampoline, where everything had been good once, where we'd all had fun, just seemed like the right place to go.

I wiggled under the fence's broken board and climbed onto the trampoline. I jumped for a few minutes, but then I stopped and sat down. It was the first time I'd been here by myself. Canaan had discovered the broken plank first. He'd told us all about it and brought us here. After that, the trampoline had always seemed like a magical place. Our secret — the boys' and mine. No one else in the neighborhood knew how to sneak through the fence. No one knew we came here. And when we did, we were always laughing.

And now I was here alone. It was the same place. The same trampoline. But it felt all wrong.

I buried my face in my knees and let myself cry — really cry — because no one could see me and because it all hurt so much.

I'm not sure how long I sat there. Or how long I cried. But I was so wrapped up in everything that I didn't even hear the Ryans' car pull into the driveway out front. I'm not sure if I've ever heard it. Maybe I did before, but Kevin was always the one to let us know, alerting us with his robot voice. Without him, I didn't even know they'd gotten home. Not until the back door opened and Teddy Ryan walked out.

"Nola?" he said.

I scrambled off the trampoline, wiping my face with

my hands and running toward the fence, my heart pounding. I heard Teddy's mother call from the house.

"Teddy? Who are you talking to? Is there somebody there?"

I'd just started shimmying through the gap when I heard Teddy yell back, "No. I was just talking to myself. No one's out here."

I had no idea why Teddy had lied to his mama. He could've gotten me in real trouble. But the damage was done. He'd seen our secret way of sneaking through the fence. Soon his parents would know, and that board would be fixed.

And Canaan would have even more reason to hate me.

# Two Summers Ago

*I'll never forget the day we first snuck into Teddy Ryan's back-yard. It was June. Me and Brian were sitting on the swings, teaching Kevin how to make dandelion crowns while Canaan kicked a soccer ball around the yard. It had rolled into the neighbor's yard a few minutes ago and he'd run off after it. I wasn't paying much attention, though. I was too focused on not breaking the stems on the dandelions we'd collected.*

*"Here you go," I said, placing the finished chain on top of Kevin's head. "A crown."*

*"I wanna make another one!" he said. He was already wearing a necklace, and so was I. We never had a lack of dandelions in our yard. In the summer, it was a sea of yellow behind the house. Mama and Richard hated them — said they were weeds — but I thought they looked more like flowers.*

*"We can make one for Brian," I said, since he was the only one without dandelion jewelry, even though he'd been helping us for the past hour. "Go pick some more dan —"*

*"Y'all!" Canaan ran up to us, panting like a thirsty dog on a hot summer day. The soccer ball was tucked under his arm, but he dropped it and grabbed my arm. "Y'all gotta see this! Come on!"*

"What is it? Is something wrong?" I asked.

"No — it's great. Come on! Brian, Kevin, ya'll, too! Come on!"

The four of us ran through our neighbors' lawns, heading toward Teddy Ryan's house. Canaan led the way, not letting go of my hand until we reached the fence.

"I was kicking the ball," he said, kneeling down and running his hand across the planks like he was looking for something. "It rolled over here and I kicked it again and it hit the fence and a board — here it is! Look!" Canaan pushed one of the fence's wooden planks and, to all of our amazement, it swung upwards.

"You broke it!" Kevin squealed. "You're gonna be in trouble."

"I didn't break it," Canaan said. "Don't be dumb. It was already broke. I just found out. And we can fit through there. You know what that means? We can use the trampoline!"

"Won't we get in trouble?" I asked.

"Not if no one catches us. Come on — they ain't home right now. I already looked."

I glanced at Brian. He was older and smarter, and even though I really wanted to play on Teddy Ryan's trampoline, I knew that if Brian said we shouldn't, he was probably right.

But Brian's eyes were shining behind his glasses, and I realized he was just as excited as Canaan was.

One by one, we wiggled under the fence. Then we all just stood there, staring at the trampoline in awe. To anyone else it was just a trampoline, but to us it was like stumbling into a fairy-tale land — new, exciting, something we'd wanted for what felt like ages. Even if we had to keep it a secret.

Canaan was the first to climb on, and then he pulled me up with him. The four of us jumped for over an hour, whooping and laughing until we were all lying on our backs, staring up at the clouds and catching our breath.

"We can't tell no one," Canaan said. "Not Felicia or anyone else from the neighborhood."

"Ain't it mean to leave them out?" I asked.

"Maybe," he said. "But we can't tell them. If they knew, they'd tell other people. Then we'd all end up getting caught. This needs to be our secret. Our place."

We all agreed and pinkie-swore that we'd never tell a soul. After that day, we snuck over to Teddy Ryan's backyard every time we saw that his parents were gone. No matter how often we were there, the trampoline never lost its magic.

# Chapter Nine

On Saturday, Mama drove me up to Grandma Lucy's house in Bunker. I was still feeling cranky about moving, but I wasn't mad at Mama anymore. I was never able to stay mad at her too long.

Before we left the duplex, I insisted on taking my bike along. I told Mama that I might need to make runs to the Dollar Store to get cleaning supplies if Grandma Lucy ran out. I guess it was a good enough excuse, because she let me load it into the trunk before we left the subdivision.

Grandma Lucy didn't act happy to see us, but we didn't take offense. She never acted happy to see nobody.

"Come on in," she said when she met us at the front door. She sounded like she'd rather us not come in, though. She didn't hug us or ask us how we'd been. She just walked back into her house and left the door open so we could follow her.

Mama glanced at me, probably wondering if I'd changed my mind about spending the day here yet. I pretended I didn't notice and just kept smiling. It didn't matter how scary or mean Grandma Lucy was. Mr. Swift was somewhere here in Bunker, and this was my only chance to track him down.

Grandma Lucy's house was spotless and it smelled like peppermint. I looked around at all the hanging pictures and little knickknacks on the shelves and tables. Even though she lived just a few miles away, in the next town over, I'd hardly visited my grandmother in years. I'd seen my daddy's parents, Mamaw and Papaw, more than I'd seen Grandma Lucy in the past few years. And they lived in Tennessee, a good two hours south of us.

She took us to the kitchen and started handing me all sorts of cleaning stuff — rags and towels and glass cleaner. Then she gave me a few garbage bags.

"You've got your work cut out for you, Fionnula."

I sighed. Grandma Lucy was the only person that called me by my full first name. Except, of course, for substitute teachers who saw my name as "Fionnula" on the roll sheet. It always made the other kids in my class laugh.

I'd been named after my great-grandma, Grandma Lucy's mama, whose parents had moved here from Ireland. I'd never met Great-Grandma Fionnula, but Mama said she was the best person she knew. Too bad she didn't have a better name.

"Nola" wasn't so bad, really, but Grandma Lucy would never call me that. No matter how hard Mama and I tried to get her to stop calling me by my full name, she just kept on. She said it was disrespectful to "cheapen" a good Irish name like that. After a while, we'd stopped arguing with her.

"Come on. No use dillydallying around," she said. "Might as well get started."

We followed Grandma Lucy back outside and out to the garage, which wasn't connected to the house like most people's garages are. It was set off to the side with a gravel path leading up to the big door. Grandma Lucy pulled out a pair of keys and walked around to the side entrance. A second later she was in the garage, hollering for Mama to help her.

When the big door was finally pushed up and open, all I could do was stare. There was no car in the garage — Grandma Lucy didn't drive anymore — but there was all sorts of other stuff. Boxes and more boxes. Folded lawn chairs set against the back wall. A dusty workbench covered in rusty tools. There was junk *everywhere*.

I swallowed and looked down at the cleaning supplies in my hands. Grandma Lucy hadn't been lying; I sure did have my work cut out for me.

"Well," Mama said, stepping out of the garage and wiping her hands on her jeans. "I oughta get going. I'm gonna sit down today and try to make a wedding budget." She kissed me on the cheek. "I'll pick you up in a few hours."

"Don't forget I gotta get my bike out of the car," I said.

"Your bike?" Grandma Lucy screeched. "Why in the lord's name did you bring your bike here, Fionnula? I'm paying you to work, not ride around the sidewalks."

"I thought it might come in handy if we ran out of cleaning supplies," I said. I could hear my voice shaking. *Get used to it*, I told myself. *This is as nice as she gets.*

I put my bike on the front porch as Mama said her good-byes. I watched her drive away, wishing, for a second, that I was going with her. But then I remembered why I was here. If I could get away for just a few minutes, I might be able to spot Mr. Swift's car. Or even see him in town.

I was here for the boys.

Grandma Lucy didn't stay out in the garage with me. She just pointed at the boxes and said, "Go through those. Take out the trash." Then she pointed at the lawn chairs. "Clean those." Then she turned to the workbench. And I saw a flash of something on her face. I don't know what it was, exactly, but when she spoke next, her voice was a little softer. "Don't touch those," she said, gesturing to the tools. "Now get to work."

I breathed a sigh of relief when she'd gone. I'd much rather be out here cleaning this mess up on my own than with her. I found an old battery-powered radio on a shelf in the back corner, and it still worked. So I tuned it to Outlaw 104 and sang along while I started to clean.

I did the lawn chairs first, scrubbing them down with the rags and some soap. They were rusty and stiff, and I was sure they'd been left out in the rain a few times too many. But I got them as clean as I could. Then I moved on to the boxes. I was curious to know what I'd find in there.

The first box was mostly garbage. Old receipts, broken TV remotes, a cracked blender. I filled up the first garbage bag real fast. The second box, though, was a little more interesting. There was some trash, of course, but most of it was stuff I knew Grandma Lucy would never want to get rid of.

There were old, beat-up stuffed animals with missing eyes and torn ears that must have been Mama's when she was little. There was a golden sash that said, in big black letters, *Miss Besser County 1959*. I did some math in my head and realized that was the year Grandma Lucy turned sixteen. Then, at the very bottom, I found a dusty photo album, stuffed full of pictures. I unfolded one of the lawn chairs, got comfortable, and started to flip through the pages.

A lot of the pictures were in black-and-white, and I didn't recognize the people in them. But a few had names and dates scribbled on the back. I found a photo of my great-grandma Fionnula from 1931. I found a picture of Grandma Lucy in an old-fashioned pink dress, wearing the sash I'd just found. Her hair was pulled up and she was smiling. I didn't hardly recognize her — she was beautiful. How had I never known she was a beauty queen?

The picture that really caught my attention, though, was one of the last in the album. In it, Grandma Lucy, orange-red hair down around her shoulders, was standing next to a man with glasses and freckles. They were both flashing big white smiles at the camera. And Grandma Lucy was holding a baby — Mama.

I stared at the man in the picture. My grandpa. I'd never met him. He passed away when Mama was in high school. She said Grandma Lucy hadn't been the same after that. I studied him closely. Mama looked like him. Which I guess I did, too, since I looked like her. And there was something real nice about his smile. You couldn't tell a whole lot from a picture, but he seemed kind, friendly . . . and really, really happy.

Grandma Lucy looked happy, too. It was hard to believe the cranky old woman who yelled all the time was the same smiling girl in these pictures.

I heard a car heading down the road and looked up so I could watch it pass by.

It was a silver Saturn.

I let out a squeak and jumped to my feet, dropping the photo album back into the box where I'd found it. I ran to the front porch to grab my bike, yelling through the screen door to Grandma Lucy that I was heading to the store to get some more trash bags. Then I pedaled as fast as I could, chasing after Mr. Swift's car.

I'd already lost sight of him by the time I got down the road, but I was pretty sure he'd been headed toward the center of Bunker. They called it "downtown," but there wasn't a whole lot there. A Walmart, a couple of little stores, and two tiny little restaurants. Not much, but enough to get people from my town heading over here every weekend to do their shopping. I'd been in this part of Bunker with Mama enough times that I knew my way around.

I rode past the hardware store and the empty playground, pedaling a little slower so I could look around for the Saturn. I was about to give up when I spotted it in the parking lot of the Country Kitchen, a little restaurant just down the street. I sped up. A woman with curly red hair, wearing a pink uniform, was climbing into the passenger's seat. I pedaled hard, trying to reach the car.

But I was too late. Once the woman was inside, the car pulled out of the lot and sped off. For a second I thought about following again, but I knew I'd never be able to keep up, and who knew where they were headed now? Instead, I decided to use my detective skills to get answers.

I left my bike in front of the restaurant and walked inside. There weren't many people in the booths, and I spotted only one waitress. She was standing behind the front counter, dressed in the same pink dress and white apron as the woman I'd just seen get into Mr. Swift's car. This woman was older, though, probably close to Grandma Lucy's age, only her hair was long and light blond with dark gray roots.

I smiled at her, and she smiled back. "What can I do for you, sweetheart?"

"I'm supposed to deliver something for one of the waitresses here." I was scrambling to come up with a story. "My aunt, actually. But I just saw her leaving the parking lot."

"What are you delivering?" the woman behind the counter asked. Her name tag was smudged, but I thought it said *Elmira*. "You can probably leave it here. I'll make sure your aunt gets it tomorrow."

"Oh, thank you," I said. "But you don't gotta do that. I was hoping to visit with her, you know? But Mama didn't know what time my aunt got off work, so I guess I just missed her."

"I guess you did," maybe-Elmira said. I couldn't tell if she was buying my story or not.

"Any chance you could tell me where she lives?" I asked.

"You don't know where your own aunt lives?" She narrowed her eyes at me.

*Uh-oh,* I thought. "Uh, well, you see, I don't live in Bunker. I'm visiting my grandma for the day. I know where my aunt lives, but I've never ridden my bike there. Could you tell me how to get there from here?"

She laughed. "Sweetheart, I don't know what you're after, but you ain't getting it from me. You haven't even said your aunt's name."

"Uh . . ."

"Go on," maybe-Elmira said, gesturing toward the door. "Either order some food or get on out of here."

I left the Country Kitchen with my shoulders slumped and my stomach aching. Maybe-Elmira hadn't yelled, but getting caught in a lie made me feel like I was in trouble. I hopped on my bike and hurried out of the parking lot as fast as I could.

I was almost back to Grandma Lucy's before I remembered the garbage bags I was supposed to be picking up and had to double-back. When I finally reached the house, Grandma Lucy was sitting on the front porch drinking lemonade.

"What took you so long?" she asked.

"Got a little lost," I lied.

I took my time cleaning for the next hour or so, going slow on purpose. Then I told Grandma Lucy that this was a two-day job, and I'd have to come back next week to finish.

"Fine," she said. "But I'm not paying you 'til it's all done."

That was all right by me. I wasn't really here for the money. I just needed more time to track down Mr. Swift. At least now I had something to work with.

# Nine Summers Ago

*My earliest memory is mostly just a snapshot.*

*I was about three. I know because I was holding Rufus, the floppy stuffed dog Mamaw and Papaw gave me for my third birthday, and his left ear hadn't been ripped off yet (that happened only a few months after I got him, according to Mama). Canaan and Brian were playing in my bedroom. Kevin wasn't born yet.*

*I remember sitting in my closet, hugging Rufus to my chest. Grandma Lucy was in the living room. She must've been talking to Mama. I don't remember seeing her, but I could hear her. I could always hear her. Her voice was loud, angry — smashing through the wall like a wrecking ball.*

*I don't remember what she was saying or why she was yelling. All I know is that I'd somehow ended up sitting in my closet, hiding, only for some reason I'd left the door open.*

*The boys stared at me for a minute, then they each stood up, walked to the closet, and sat down. One boy on each side of me. I don't think they said a word. If they did, I don't recall. As far as I can remember, they just sat on the floor with me while Grandma Lucy hollered in the next room.*

*Even back then, I felt safe with the boys. They could tell when I was upset, when I needed them.*

*Who knows how long we actually sat in that closet. The memory is only about three seconds long. But I've thought about it a million times over the years. One little memory. One tiny moment. But I think that's really where our friendship began.*

# Chapter Ten

I nearly tripped over Kevin on my way out the door Thursday morning. He was sitting on the top step, just waiting for me.

"You don't knock no more, either?" I asked.

He lifted one shoulder, then let it drop.

"Well, I can't play right now," I told him. "I've got to go walk Mrs. Santos's dog and water Miss Shirley's flowers."

He hopped to his feet and looked up at me, hands shoved in his pockets.

"You wanna help?" I guessed.

He nodded.

"Fine by me." I locked the front door and jumped down the steps. "It'll be nice to have some company, I suppose."

I didn't tell him I'd been looking for Mr. Swift. I didn't wanna say anything until I actually found him. Or maybe I'd never say nothing. Maybe I'd just convince him to come home and let him surprise the boys. They'd never have to know I was a part of it.

Kevin was glued to my side all day. I didn't mind, of course, but sometimes, whenever I wasn't talking, I'd just sorta look at him and feel my heart break. It was hard to believe that just a few weeks ago, everything was different. Kevin didn't even feel like Kevin anymore.

"You coming over?" I asked him once I'd finished with Miss Shirley's garden.

He nodded.

We walked back down the street, toward the duplex. We passed Mr. Briggs's house. He waved to us when we walked by.

"Afternoon, kids," he said.

"Good afternoon, Mr. Briggs," I called back. Kevin waved.

Back at my house, we sat on the living room floor and

played Chutes and Ladders while we waited for Mama to get home. I'd brought Kevin a notebook and a blue marker, too, so he could write out anything he might want to say. Which wasn't much, actually.

"Hey, kiddos," Richard said when he and Mama walked through the door that night. "Who's winning?"

"Kevin," I grumbled.

"Nice job, Kevster," Richard said.

Kevin smiled, and that made me feel a little less grouchy about losing.

"You should let your mama know if you're staying for dinner," I told him.

He reached for the marker and scribbled on the paper I'd given him. Then he passed it to me. In messy handwriting, it said:

Mamas at work.

"Well, you should tell Brian, then," I said.

Dont no ware Brian is.

I stared down at the paper. "What do you mean you don't know where Brian is? He ain't at home?"

He visted Ty last week. He dynt bin home sinse thin. He calls mama evry day, tho.

119

It didn't make much sense to me. Brian hadn't been home since last week? It was hard to believe he'd been away from home that long. Especially when he seemed to be the one keeping an eye on Canaan and Kevin. I didn't say anything like that, though. I just nodded and we finished our game.

Later that night, after dinner, Kevin and me were sitting out on the front steps. It was getting around time for him to go home, but I could tell he was stalling — or "procrastinating," as Richard would remind me to say. My notebook and marker were in his lap, and after a few minutes of listening to the crickets chirp, I finally asked something I'd been wondering for weeks.

"Kevin . . . how come you don't talk no more?"

He picked up the marker, like he was going to write, but then it just hovered in the air. After a long pause, he sighed and shook his head. He handed me the notebook and the marker before giving me a quick hug. Then, with a tiny wave, he got to his feet and walked home.

*　*　*

Felicia asked me to spend the night at her house on Friday. I packed my sleeping bag, toothbrush, and pajamas in an old pink backpack and walked across the street just before suppertime. Mrs. Hooper had a plate of steak and a baked potato already waiting on the table for me.

After we ate, me and Felicia watched movies in her living room while we played MASH — a game that tells your future and whether or not you'll end up living in a mansion, apartment, shack, or house. When I first learned the game in fourth grade, I took my results very seriously. It wasn't just a game — it was as good as gospel. Obviously, since then I'd figured out that the results were different every time, which meant they couldn't really be true. It was still fun, though.

"Okay," Felicia said, picking up the sheet of paper we'd used for her turn. "So I'm gonna live in a house. I'm gonna have three kids. My wedding dress will be green." She made a face — the same one she got whenever she had to scoop after JW on a walk. "And I'm gonna marry Canaan. . . . Not too bad."

"Nope," I mumbled. So I knew it was a dumb game, but I was a little jealous. Partly because I always thought I'd be the one marrying Canaan, and right now we weren't even talking. And partly because, in the game

I'd just played, I'd ended up living in a shack married to Teddy Ryan.

"All right, girls," Mrs. Hooper said. "You don't have to go to sleep, but it's time to get pajamas on and go to Felicia's room."

Felicia whined a little, but she ended up falling asleep real quick. It couldn't have been five minutes after her pajamas were on that she started snoring.

I wasn't tired, though. Not yet. I sat on Felicia's windowsill, the notepad we'd used to play MASH in my lap. I was using the light from the streetlamp outside to draw pictures. I was working on a sketch of JW, who was curled up, asleep at the foot of Felicia's bed. It was turning out to be a pretty good drawing and I thought Felicia would probably like it. Maybe she'd tack it to her wall, put it up behind the little wooden statue Mr. Briggs had given her, which I'd seen sitting on her dresser.

I'd just started on JW's tail when I noticed something out of the corner of my eye. There were three people outside, standing on the corner. I couldn't see their faces, just their silhouettes. I pressed my face to the window, trying to see what they were doing, but as far as I could tell, they were just standing. Talking, maybe.

A second later, they moved, all of them turning to walk up the street. When they passed under the streetlight, I got a quick look at their faces.

Andy Kirk and Peter Miller — the biggest bullies in the neighborhood — and they were with Canaan.

For a minute, I just stared — confused. Canaan *hated* Andy and Peter. They used to sneak into the backyard and tip over our swing set. They were the boys who picked on the younger kids. The boys who pulled up the flowers in Miss Shirley's garden just for the sake of meanness. Why was he with them?

I decided I was gonna find out.

I climbed off the windowsill and tiptoed across the room to my shoes. JW woke up, sniffed, and turned his dark eyes toward me. I put a finger to my lips and said, "Shhh." Then I felt silly because of course a dog wouldn't understand what that meant.

I pulled on my sandals and slid, quietly, out of Felicia's bedroom.

I wasn't sure how late it was, but Felicia's parents had

already gone to bed. I crept through the dark living room and opened the front door slowly, hoping it wouldn't creak. Once I was outside, though, I had to move fast to catch up.

They were still headed up the street. I could hear them talking and laughing. I stayed back, keeping to the shadows so they wouldn't turn around and spot me following them. They all must have snuck out of their houses, and I wanted to know what they were up to.

"So, who should it be?" I heard Andy ask. He was holding something in his hand, but I couldn't see what.

"That one," Peter said. It was hard to tell, but I thought he was pointing at Mrs. Santos's house. "I hate that woman. Her and her stupid dog."

"What do you think, Canaan?" Andy asked.

"Fine by me," he said. His voice was flat, like he didn't really care either way. "Apathetic," Richard would say.

"Let me do it." Peter grabbed for the thing in Andy's hand.

"You'll mess it up," Andy said, keeping whatever-it-was out of Peter's grasp.

They'd stopped now, in the middle of the sidewalk, right in front of Mrs. Santos's house. I crouched down and hid in the bushes across the street, watching.

"Canaan, you wanna do it?" Andy asked.

"Why does he get to?" Peter whined. "He ain't never done it before. Plus, he'll mess it up!"

"I can do it," Canaan said.

Andy handed the thing to him.

Canaan gave it a shake before stepping up next to Mrs. Santos's mailbox. That's when I realized what he was holding.

A spray paint can.

The other boys stood back, watching while Canaan sprayed something onto the mailbox. A few seconds later, he was done, and they stepped forward to check out his work.

"Not bad," Andy said.

"I could've done it better," Peter huffed.

"Let's get out of here," Canaan said, handing the can back to Andy.

They headed back in the other direction, moving quieter and quicker this time. I held my breath and sat real still, but they didn't see me. They stayed on the opposite side of the street. Once they were gone, I slipped out from behind the bushes and walked over to Mrs. Santos's yard.

On the side of her mailbox were four bright red let-ters. Letters that spelled out a word any one of those boys' mamas would have tanned their hide for using.

I felt bad for Mrs. Santos. She'd wake up to that word, staring at her when she checked her morning mail. She'd probably have to get it painted over, and that'd cost money. If it was just Andy and Peter, I would've told on them. I knew their parents would make them find a way to pay for it. But Canaan had been the one to do it, and there was no way I could tell on him. No matter how bad things had gotten.

There was nothing I could do to fix it, either.

I walked back to Felicia's, feeling sad and angry all at once. I couldn't believe Canaan would do that. I couldn't believe he was friends with Andy and Peter now.

Friends with Andy and Peter, but not with me.

There was a time when he'd defended me against those boys. When we were in third grade and they'd started calling me names like "Nasty Nola." They'd told stories about me having lice and smelling like a skunk. None of it was true, of course, but that didn't stop some people from believing it. One day, when they were fol-lowing me around the playground saying things like

"Do you smell that?" and "I can see bugs all over her!" Canaan stepped in. He'd shoved Peter, sending him toppling backwards into Andy.

"Leave her alone, or else!" he'd yelled.

He'd lost recess privileges for a week after that. But he'd said he didn't care, because it got the boys to stop bothering me.

How could that be the same boy who was running around with Andy and Peter in the middle of the night, spray-painting people's mailboxes now?

I slipped back into Felicia's bedroom, took off my shoes, and climbed into my sleeping bag. I missed Canaan. Not this new, mean Canaan, but the one I'd grown up with. My best friend. It felt like he'd vanished overnight and hadn't bothered to say good-bye.

Kinda like his daddy had done, I guess.

Just like at the birthday party, I think JW sensed I was upset. He hopped off Felicia's bed curled up next to me, his tail wagging softly. I reached out and scratched his ears. Then I fell asleep with his cold, wet nose pressed against my cheek.

# Last Summer

*Mama said I could have a sleepover at our house. I'd wanted to invite the boys, but earlier that week Mama had sat me down and told me that I was eleven years old and that was a little too old to have boys sleep over anymore. So I'd invited Felicia instead.*

*Felicia was my closest friend that was a girl, and even though I'd have rather been with the boys, I knew having her spend the night would be fun, too.*

*We watched movies and ate candy and Mama let us borrow her nail polish to paint each other's toenails. Once our nails were bright pink, Felicia turned to me and looked me right in the eye.*

*"Truth or dare?" she asked me.*

*"Truth," I said. I was too scared to pick dare.*

*"If you could marry anyone in the world, who would you pick?"*

*"I don't know," I said.*

*"You gotta answer," Felicia told me. "Or else you face Consequences."*

*"What's Consequences?"*

*"Like, a real big dare. Something you really won't want to do. Like . . . eat ketchup on a cinnamon roll or something."*

"Eww. That's gross, Felicia."

"That's Consequences. So you better answer. Come on. Who would you marry?"

I looked down at my hands in my lap, feeling embarrassed. "Well . . . Canaan, I guess."

Felicia clapped her hands together, her dark brown eyes brightening. "You like Canaan? You got a crush on him?"

I shook my head. "No. I don't." And I didn't. It wasn't that I wanted to grow up and marry Canaan. I'd just always figured that's how it would be. We'd get married and buy a house and Kevin and Brian would live in houses on either side of us, and we'd always be together just like we were now.

"Then why would you marry him?" Felicia asked, stretching out on her stomach and staring up at me with her chin in her hands.

"Because he's my best friend," I said, shrugging. "I think it'd be nice to marry your best friend."

"Maybe," Felicia said. "But I'd rather marry a movie star. Or a writer — someone who could write me all the books I want for free."

"That'd be nice, too," I said. But really, I didn't care about any of that. If I was gonna spend every day with someone, I wanted it to be Canaan.

# Chapter Eleven

Canaan was dribbling a basketball in the Swifts' empty driveway the next morning when I walked back from Felicia's house. I almost walked past him. I almost made it all the way to my front door without saying a word. But then I thought about those red letters and the spray paint can in Canaan's hand, and I just couldn't stop myself.

"Why'd you do it?"

He didn't even stop dribbling. "Do what?"

"I saw you last night," I said. "I saw what you and those other boys did to Mrs. Santos's mailbox. Why were you hanging out with them?"

"You gonna rat on us?"

"I thought about it, but . . . no. Even though I should."

"Then mind your own business." He threw the basketball onto the ground and let it bounce off into the grass. I watched him stomp his way up the front steps and slam through the front door.

I sighed.

Mama was waiting for me inside. She looked up from a bridal magazine when I walked in.

"I'm ready to go," I told her.

"You don't *have* to, you know," she said, putting the magazine aside. "Normally I'd never encourage you to quit in the middle of a job, but I know how nervous Grandma Lucy makes you."

"I'll be all right."

"Are you sure?" she asked. "You've always hated visiting her. It's just a little odd that you're so eager to help her out all of a sudden."

I shrugged. "I don't know. I guess I changed my mind? She's not going to be around forever, you know. I should get to know her while I can." It was a nice thing to say, even if it wasn't entirely true. Which made me feel sorta bad. But I didn't think Mama would take well to my search for Mr. Swift.

"That's sweet," she said. "Oh, Nola Baby. I wish your

Mamaw and Papaw lived closer. Your daddy's parents are some of the best people I know. You know I love your grandma Lucy, but those are the grandparents I really wish you could spend more time with."

"I wish that, too," I said. "But Grandma Lucy lives close by, so . . ."

"You're such a good girl. I'm her daughter, and I wouldn't even volunteer to spend my Saturdays with her." She stood up and stretched her arms over her head. "All right. Let's go, then. You know how your grandma hates to be kept waiting."

I had a plan before we even got to Bunker. I was gonna say my hellos to Grandma Lucy, finish up the garage, and then ride my bike to the Country Kitchen. Hopefully, this time, I'd be able to get more information. There were a few dollars in my pocket so that I could order something and maybe-Elmira wouldn't kick me out.

"So you're back."

That was Grandma Lucy's version of a greeting.

"Good to see you, too, Mother. Nola's really looking forward to spending the day with you, you know," Mama said.

"Well, I'm looking forward to having a clean garage."

I could tell Mama was getting frustrated, so I cut in.

"I'll get started right away, Grandma Lucy. Sorry I wasn't able to finish last week." I grabbed the cleaning supplies she'd left on the kitchen counter for me. "I'll just let you know when I'm done."

"Fine," Grandma Lucy said. "And remember — don't you touch that workbench, Fionnula."

"Yes, ma'am."

Mama walked back outside with me and helped me open the garage door. "That workbench," she said, sighing as she stared at the wooden table and dirty tools. "She hasn't let anyone put a hand on those tools since the day my daddy died."

"I found a bunch of pictures in that box over there," I said, pointing. "There were some of her and Grandpa together. And one of her in a beauty pageant."

"Oh yeah," Mama said. "Did I never tell you about that? Your grandmother used to be known as the prettiest girl in Besser County."

"She looked real happy in all those pictures," I said. "The one from the pageant and all the others — with Grandpa and you as a baby."

"She used to be different. Before he passed away."

She shook her head. "Anyway. I oughta get going. I'll be back in a few hours. And I'll put your bike on the front porch in case you need to go get anything." She kissed my cheek. "Bye, baby."

"Bye."

There wasn't a whole lot left to do in the garage, just some organizing and sweeping. I turned on the radio and got to work. I threw out the rest of the junk and grabbed the broom, which looked like it was older than me by the way the bristles were ripped and bent. It still worked all right, though. There was a Miranda Lambert song on, and I couldn't help singing along.

But maybe I was having a little too much fun. I started dancing around, singing into the end of the broomstick and pretending I was on the stage at the Grand Ole Opry. I should've been paying more attention, though. I shouldn't have been goofing off. Because I was belting out the chorus and I spun around with the broom and —

I tripped.

I tripped and I fell right into the workbench full of tools. About half of them fell onto the concrete floor, clattering in a way that made me cringe and squeak. I kicked the broom aside and scrambled to pick up the tools, terrified Grandma Lucy would come out to check on me right at that minute and yell at me for messing with the bench.

Most of the tools were fine and I was able to put them back right where I'd found them. But one, an old yellow drill, hadn't held up so well. There was a crack running along the bottom side, and a piece near the bit had broken off completely.

I almost started crying right then and there.

I tried to put it back together, but it was no use. The drill was broken. I set it back on the workbench and tried to make it look like it was still together. If Grandma Lucy saw — if she knew I'd broke it — she'd kill me. I'd be in so much trouble.

There wasn't much left for me to do in the garage, and all I really wanted was to get away from the tools. So I figured now was a good time to head down to the Country Kitchen and look for the waitress. I took the cleaning supplies back inside the house. Grandma Lucy was folding clothes in the living room. "Done already, Fionnula?" she asked.

"Y-yes, ma'am." I was so scared she was going to yell. Like she could look at me and just know what I'd done. I knew I should tell her, but the idea of admitting that the drill was broken, especially after she'd repeatedly told me to stay away from the tools, made me feel like throwing up.

"I ain't paying you if you did a sloppy job."

I swallowed. "I did my best."

"We'll see." She folded the last shirt in her basket and stood up from the couch. "Your mother won't be back for a while. What are you gonna do until then?"

"Um, I was getting hungry, so I thought I might ride my bike down to that little diner — the Country Kitchen? I saw it when I was getting trash bags the other day. It looked nice."

"It's all right, I reckon," Grandma Lucy said. "Nothing special."

I wasn't sure what I was supposed to say to that. So I just sort of stood there for a second, chewing on my lip and trying to figure out if I was allowed to go now or if I should wait for permission. I was still fighting the urge to take off out the door at a run.

She put her basket away and carried the clean clothes to her bedroom. When she came back she said, "I'm hungry, too. I might as well go with you."

"W-what?" I stammered, feeling panicky.

"It's not far. We can walk," she said, pulling a wide-brimmed straw hat over her short gray curls. "And a chicken salad sounds good right about now."

So we walked down to the restaurant together. It was about half a mile from her house, but Grandma Lucy didn't walk too fast and she got mad and scolded me when I got too far ahead of her. By the time we got to the restaurant, I felt like I was about to throw up from nerves.

Maybe-Elmira wasn't standing behind the register today. Instead there was a pregnant woman with big green eyes and black hair. "Y'all eating here or is it to go?" she asked.

"Here," I said.

"Sit anywhere you like. Sarah will be right with you."

Grandma Lucy picked a booth next to the far window. I slid into the seat across from her and started looking around the restaurant, hoping I'd catch sight of the redhead I'd seen Mr. Swift leave with last week. I also wanted a reason to keep from looking at Grandma Lucy. I felt my lip trembling every time I looked her in the eye.

"For God's sake, Fionnula. Put your behind in the seat," she hissed. "You're twelve years old — you oughta know how to sit properly."

"Sorry, Grandma Lucy," I mumbled. I hadn't even realized I'd been half standing while I craned my neck around. But when you're like me — not real tall at all — it's hard to see over the back of these booths without standing up. Again, I felt like I was in trouble, and I felt sicker than I did a few minutes ago.

"Hello, hello," a voice chirped above my head. I looked up and almost gasped.

There was the woman with the curly red hair. She was wearing the same pink uniform, and the name tag clipped to her shirt said *Sarah*. Up close, I could tell how pretty she was. She had blue eyes and a big, straight-toothed smile.

"How are y'all today?" she asked in a cheerful, fluttery voice.

"All right, I guess," Grandma Lucy said.

Sarah handed us each a menu. "Can I go ahead and get your drink orders?"

"Dr Pepper," I said.

Grandma Lucy huffed. "That garbage will rot your teeth."

I bit my lip. "Um . . . Or just water."

"Lemonade for me," Grandma Lucy said. "Is it homemade?"

"Sure is, ma'am," Sarah said, scribbling our orders on a little notepad. "I'll be right back with those drinks."

I wanted to point out that lemonade had a lot of sugar, too, but I didn't want to get in trouble, so I kept my mouth shut. Maybe when you were old, you didn't care so much about your own teeth, just other people's.

When Sarah'd gone, Grandma Lucy heaved and groaned her way out of the booth. "I've gotta use the ladies' room. I'll be back. If she comes for our order, I want the chicken salad without dressing."

I nodded.

I started flipping through the menu, but I wasn't really reading it. I was too jumpy, worried about the drill and trying to figure out how I was going to get information about Mr. Swift with Grandma Lucy here. It might not be possible. And that would make this whole afternoon a waste.

"Here you are." Sarah appeared with our drinks. She put down Grandma Lucy's lemonade, then turned to me. "I brought you Dr Pepper," she whispered. "Just tell her I got your order wrong, and it's my fault."

"Thank you," I said.

"No problem," she said. "I had a mean grandmother once, too."

And that's when I saw my opportunity. Grandma Lucy wasn't back yet and Sarah was here, and if I did this quick enough —

"You know, I think you know my . . . my uncle," I said, cobbling the lie together as fast as my brain would let me. "David Swift?"

"You're David's niece?" she exclaimed. "Oh my goodness, it's so lovely to meet you! Wait . . . That woman's not his mother, right?"

"Oh no," I said. "That's my grandmother on my mama's side. Mr. — uh, Uncle David is related to me on my daddy's side."

"Oh, thank God," she said. "I would not want her to be my mother-in-law."

"Mother-in-law?" I asked.

"Well . . ." She blushed. "He hasn't proposed just yet, but we are living together now, so . . . I figure it's just a matter of time."

My heart sank.

"Oh, but don't mention it to your family or any-thing," she said quickly. "I haven't gotten to meet a lot of them just yet, and like I said, he hasn't proposed or anything. That was a stupid thing to say a minute ago — I shouldn't have even said it. Anyway, I'm Sarah Clarke. It's nice to meet you —"

I was saved from having to make up a name when Grandma Lucy, back from the bathroom, squeezed back into the booth. I ducked my head. After everything I'd just heard from Sarah on top of what had happened with the drill, I was feeling just plain rotten. "You're here," she said to Sarah. "Good. I want the chicken salad. No dressing."

"Got it," Sarah said. "And for you?"

"Um . . . just a hamburger, please."

"Okay. It'll be right out."

Sarah hurried away. I just sat there, staring at the table. Mr. Swift was living with that woman. He might even marry her. I knew these kinds of things hap-pened — I'd seen enough daytime television to know all about it — but I still didn't understand. Mr. Swift had left without saying good-bye to his wife or kids. Just up and left and never came back. And this whole time, he was living in Bunker, with a waitress named Sarah Clarke who thought they were getting married.

"Fionnula?" Grandma Lucy's voice was surprisingly soft. "You don't look so well."

"I'm okay," I murmured. But I wasn't.

There was a long stretch of silence, then Grandma Lucy said, "I'm sorry."

I looked up, not sure I believed what I'd just heard. "Huh?"

"Don't make me say it again," she grunted. "I know I'm cross when I shouldn't be, and your mama's always told me how sensitive you are. And, well . . . I'm sorry. It's not personal."

I nodded. It was the first apology — and probably the last — I'd ever get from my grandmother. But it only made me feel worse. I owed her the apology for breaking the drill, but I was too much of a coward to tell her.

Nothing I'd done was as bad as Mr. Swift, though. If anyone deserved an apology right now, it was Mrs. Swift and the boys. I just wondered how long it would take them to get one.

# Chapter Twelve

The next day, Sunday, was the Fourth of July. I woke up to the sound of firecrackers down the street, and for the first time in my life, it didn't make me smile. I'd had nightmares all night, dreaming about getting yelled at by Grandma Lucy and about being chased by someone with a yellow drill and about chasing Mr. Swift's silver Saturn. I groaned and rolled over, pulling my pillow over my head. That didn't work for long, though.

"Nola Baby," Mama called as she knocked on my bedroom door. "Someone's here to see you."

"Who?" I yelled.

"Why don't you be polite by coming out here to find

out yourself," she suggested in that way that meant it wasn't a suggestion at all.

I kicked off my blanket and stomped into the living room. I didn't know who to expect, but definitely not Teddy Ryan. There he was, sitting on my couch, looking fidgety and nervous. His head bobbed up when he heard me walk in the room.

My hand flew to my hair — which had to be a mess — and I suddenly felt self-conscious about the shorts and T-shirt I'd fallen asleep in. And I didn't even have on a training bra. I folded my arms over my chest. Not that I cared what Teddy Ryan thought. It would've been embarrassing to greet anyone looking like this.

"Hi, Nola," he said.

"Hey," I said. "How are you?"

"I'm fine, thanks."

"Teddy's parents are going to the fireworks tonight," Mama said.

"Oh," I said. I wasn't sure why she was bothering to tell me this. Nearly everybody in town went to the fireworks. People would park all up and down Main Street, then walk down to the river. Some people brought tables and chairs. Others sat on blankets. And everybody smelled like mosquito repellent. Going to the fireworks wasn't special. It was expected.

"Yeah." Teddy nodded and fiddled with his glasses. "We're going tonight, and, uh, I was wondering . . . do you wanna come with us?"

*That*, however, was not expected.

"Come with you to the fireworks?" I asked.

"Uh-huh," Teddy said. "Daddy's gonna pack us a picnic. They said I could bring a friend along, and I thought . . . Well, I decided to ask you. So do you wanna come?"

I couldn't remember the last time I'd been to the fireworks with anyone but the Swifts. The boys and me would always sit on the dock, our feet dangling in the dirty river water while we watched the bursts of color dance over our heads. That's how it was every year.

But things had changed. More than I'd even realized, if Teddy Ryan considered me a friend now.

"I guess so," I said. "That could be all right."

"Nola," Mama whispered to me. "A little more enthusiasm?"

But it was enough for Teddy. He gave me a big grin, like I'd just made his day, and hopped off the couch.

"Great. We're leaving at eight thirty. Do you want us to pick you up?"

"Nah. I can walk to your house," I said.

But when eight thirty came, Teddy Ryan was waiting on my front porch, wearing that same goofy grin. "I thought we could walk over to my house together," he said.

"Oh, all right."

"Have fun, kids," Mama said. "Richard and I will be around, but we promise not to bother y'all." She leaned down, kissed my cheek, and whispered, "You look beautiful."

"Thanks." I didn't know why she bothered to say that. It was nice of her, but I was just wearing blue jean cutoffs and a red tank top. My hair was barely fixed — I'd pulled it up into a messy bun. I wasn't trying to look beautiful — I just didn't want to sweat to death outside.

Me and Teddy walked down the street together, not saying nothing for a while. Then he said, "Just so you know, I didn't tell my parents."

"Tell your parents what?" I asked.

"About the trampoline," he said. "I didn't tell them."

"Oh . . . So the fence?"

He shook his head. "I didn't tell them," he repeated. "And, if you ever wanna sneak into our backyard again, you can. . . . Or you can just come to the front door. Then we can jump together."

"Oh . . . Thank you," I said.

Teddy's parents were loading up the car with folding chairs and blankets. "Hello, Nola," Mrs. Ryan said. She was a real pretty black woman with skin a few shades darker than Teddy's and the exact same big, goofy smile. "We're so glad you're coming with us tonight."

"Thanks for inviting me," I said.

Mr. Ryan shut the trunk and walked around to the front of the car. He was tall and thin with light skin and hair that reminded me of Edna's at Rocky's — very ghostly. But his eyes were a light hazel, just like Teddy's, and he wore thick, round glasses like him, too. "All right," he said. "We're all set. Pile in."

Neither Teddy or me said anything on the way to the river. Mr. and Mrs. Ryan did all the talking — and they talked a lot: about the songs on the radio, about the food they'd packed, about last year's fireworks and their hopes for this year. The car stayed full of chatter, right up until Mrs. Ryan parallel-parked on the side of Main Street.

We helped Mr. Ryan unload the trunk, each of us carrying something down the hill toward the riverbank. I could already smell charcoal and barbecue, hear country music blasting from battery-powered radios, see the sun setting, way off in the distance, behind the trees across the water. It was so pretty. I tried to take a picture in my head, to memorize it so I could draw it later.

We picked a spot close to the dock and settled in, spreading the blanket and unfolding the chairs. Mr. Ryan started passing out sandwiches right away, which I was grateful for since Mama and I had eaten only a small dinner and I was already hungry again.

"I hope you like PB and J," Mr. Ryan said, handing me a sandwich in a plastic bag.

"I do," I said. "Thank you very much."

"And here's yours, Teddy."

Teddy took his sandwich. I couldn't see what it was, but the frown on his face told me it wasn't very exciting. That's when I remembered Felicia's birthday party and the food allergies he'd told me about. I felt a little bad for him.

Mr. and Mrs. Ryan went off to talk with some of their friends, who were setting up camp a few yards away.

Without them, things got real quiet. Teddy and me sat on the blanket, eating our sandwiches and waiting for it to get dark enough for the fireworks to start.

"So," Teddy said, finally breaking the silence. "How has your summer been so far?"

"Um . . . Not great, really."

"Why? What's wrong?"

"It's complicated."

"Oh." Teddy nibbled at his sandwich — which I could see had a lot of green leafy vegetables poking out from between the slices of bread. Ew.

"What about yours?" I asked.

"All right," he said. "My aunt got a pool, so I've been over at her house a lot."

"Lucky," I said. "I've always wanted a pool. I've begged Mama to get one for years."

"You could come to my aunt's with me sometime," he said. He looked down at his lap. "I wouldn't mind."

Before I could answer, there was an explosion over our heads. We looked up and watched as green and blue and pink sparks flew out in every direction. We stopped talking for a while and just watched the fireworks. They were beautiful — stars and flowers in every color.

Usually I loved the fireworks, but this year, watching them just made me feel sad.

Last year, the boys and I sat on the dock while Mama, Richard, and Mrs. Swift sat at a picnic table, playing cards and talking. Mr. Swift was there, too, grilling burgers for everybody and listening while the boys and me told him jokes. He didn't laugh as much as we wanted him to, but that was all right. We all ate and sang along to the radio and skipped rocks on the river. Then Brian spotted a few of his friends and Kevin got tired, so he went up the hill to sit in his mama's lap, and it was just me and Canaan on the dock, watching the fireworks.

"You know what?" Canaan had said, standing up. "It's hot."

"It's summer," I'd replied. "It's supposed to be hot."

He'd pulled off his T-shirt then.

"What are you doing?" But I don't know why I'd bothered asking. I knew.

Canaan backed up, then he took a running jump right off the dock and into the river. The splash was timed perfectly with the next explosion of fireworks, and it left me dripping wet. Canaan sputtered and laughed as he treaded water, his head bobbing on the same level as my knees.

"You coming?" he'd asked.

"No," I'd said. "Your mama's gonna kill you for jumping in there."

"It's all right. She'll get over it." He swam around in a circle before disappearing under the water. I watched the surface, the light from the fireworks dancing across the ripples, expecting him to come up for air at any second.

Then something grabbed hold of my ankle, and I screamed, my brain conjuring up images of snakes and river monsters. Things that would drag me under and eat me alive.

"That's not funny!" I'd yelled as Canaan's head burst up from the water, his mouth wide and laughing. "You scared me half to death! I could've fallen in! Oh, lord — I thought you were a snake or something worse."

"Oh, come on, Nola," he'd said. "You know I'd never let you drown. Or let a snake get a hold of you."

I'd snorted. "What could you do against a snake, Canaan Swift?"

"Don't know," he'd admitted. "But I'd find a way to fight him off. That's what best-best friends are for, right?"

"For fighting off snakes?"

"Yeah," he'd said. "And for saving each other from drowning."

I'd laughed. I'd laughed a lot that night last year. I'd laughed when Canaan made a show of diving under-water each time the fireworks went off. I'd laughed when Mrs. Swift had stormed down to the dock and demanded he get back on dry land. I'd laughed the whole way home, sitting in the backseat of Mama's car with Canaan, who was soaked and shivering, wrapped inside in a towel.

"Not so hot now, is it?" I'd teased.

But that was twelve long months ago, and tonight, sitting crisscrossed on the blanket next to Teddy Ryan, I suddenly didn't feel so much like laughing.

I felt Teddy shift beside me. His hand brushed mine and I turned to look at him. He was looking at me already, his hazel eyes wide behind those thick glasses. He had real nice eyes. I looked down; his fingers lightly

touched mine. That's when I realized it wasn't no accident, and I wasn't sure how I felt about that.

I looked up again, not sure if I was gonna say something or just smile back — and then I saw them, over
Teddy's shoulder.

Three boys, standing in a huddle, hands in their
pockets. Andy, Peter, and Canaan. They were about ten
yards away, but they weren't looking at us. Their heads
were together, like they were whispering to each other.
Like they were planning.

Teddy turned his head to see what I was looking at. "Oh," he said, his voice low. "I wonder what
they're up to."

"So do I," I mumbled.

"Kids like that are the reason my parents put up a
fence," he said.

I shook my head. "Canaan ain't like them," I insisted.
"He's not like Andy and Peter."

"You sure?" Teddy asked.

I started to say "Yes!" to tell him that I was sure, that
Canaan was different, to get mad at him for even sug-
gesting he could be like them.

But I remembered the red letters on Mrs. Santos's mailbox. Angry letters in an angry word. And truth was, I wasn't sure. Not anymore. I didn't know this Canaan.

The boys pulled apart and started walking down the bank, away from us. Canaan hung back a step. He turned his head, and I swear, he looked right at me. At me and Teddy Ryan, sitting together. For a second I thought he'd come over. For a second, I thought he'd say something.

He didn't.

"You coming?" I heard Peter yell.

"Yeah," Canaan called. He looked at me a second longer, then he turned away and started walking, moving quick so he could catch up with the other boys.

"Nola?" Teddy said. He was looking at me, not the boys' retreating backs. "You okay?"

"Huh?" I said. "Yeah . . . Yeah, I'm all right."

"Do you want another sandwich?" he asked. "We packed extras in the cooler."

I shook my head. "Nah. I'm good. Thank you, though."

"Okay . . . Hey, Nola?"

"Yeah?"

"Can I tell you something?"

"Sure."

"Before, when I put gum in your hair and kicked your seat on the bus — I wasn't trying to be mean or pick on you or nothing," he said.

"Then why'd you do that stuff?" I asked.

He looked awful embarrassed, tugging on the collar of his striped shirt and fixing his glasses again. "Well, I was just . . . I wanted to get your attention. So we could be friends."

I almost laughed. "If you wanna be friends, that sure ain't the way to do it, Teddy. You should've just said hi."

"I tried," he insisted. "But every time I did, Canaan would start yelling at me and you'd just walk away or turn your head, so I . . . kicked your seat. Or stuck gum in your hair. I didn't know how else to make you pay attention. So . . . I'm sorry."

It might have been funny or even sweet to hear him say that, but it just made me think of all the times Canaan ran him off. Canaan didn't know no better — he just thought Teddy was trying to be mean and he wanted to protect me. He always tried to protect me.

Not anymore, though.

"Nola?" Teddy asked. "You okay? Did you hear me? I said I was sorry."

"I heard you," I said. "And thank you. I accept your apology."

"So do you think we could maybe be friends?"

I nodded. "Of course." And, after a second, I realized I meant it. Even though part of me wished I was there with the Swift boys, the way it used to be, Teddy Ryan was pretty good company, too. And now that I knew he wasn't mean after all, I thought I might like being friends with him.

We watched the rest of the fireworks together, talking in little, random spurts. He asked me about the teachers in the sixth grade, and I told him Mr. Bryant, the science teacher, had a hamster in his room named Pluto. He told me he was learning to play the cello, but he was really bad at it. I asked him what a cello was because I'd never heard of one. And we both laughed a few times, smiled a few more.

Teddy didn't move his hand the whole time, and I didn't move mine, neither.

# Chapter Thirteen

I rode my bike up to Rocky's by myself on Monday. I was still doing a couple jobs around the subdivision, but I wasn't hunting so hard for them no more. I had quite a bit of money saved up already. Definitely enough for the circus tickets. Though I wasn't sure why I was still thinking about that, with the way things were going between me and the boys. I wanted to hold out hope, but I couldn't help feeling a ball of anger burning in my belly every time I thought of them leaving me hanging like this.

Edna was happy to see me. She smiled when I walked in. "Nola," she said, smacking the counter. "My favorite customer. I hear your mama got engaged."

"Yes, ma'am. She did," I said.

"Tell her congratulations for me."

"I sure will," I said. "She's very happy."

"Good, good. Well, what can I do for you today, darling?"

"Can I get a peanut-butter milkshake, please? And French fries." I knew they'd be soggy, but I was hungry, and they were better than a burnt burger.

"You surely can."

I paid for my order and took a seat at one of the booths. A few minutes later, Edna brought my food out to me. "I brought some extra ketchup packets for you," she said. "And let me know when you're done. . . . , There just might be a dessert waiting for you. On the house."

"You don't gotta do that, Edna," I said.

"You're right," she said. "I don't gotta, but I can." She squeezed my shoulder. "Enjoy your meal, all right?"

"Thank you."

I'd just ripped open one of those ketchup packets when the bells over the door jingled again. I glanced over my shoulder and had to bite my lip to keep from gasping. It was Andy, Peter, and Canaan. They were being loud — laughing and shoving at each other the way boys do. They didn't even say a word to Edna, just went straight to a booth and sat down.

"Can I get y'all anything?" Edna called to them from behind the counter.

"We're still thinking about what we want," Andy said. "We'll let you know."

I kept my head down, focusing all my attention on the soggy French fries in front of me. I wanted to be mad at Canaan. I wanted to walk right over to that booth, take him by the shoulders, and shake him. I wanted to scream and yell and ask him what the heck he was thinking, hanging out with boys like that.

But I couldn't. I remembered Sarah and what she'd said about Mr. Swift — that they were living together, that they might get married. When I remembered that, all I could feel for Canaan was sorry.

I could feel the boys' eyes on me. It made me squirm, but I still kept my eyes down. Then I heard one of them moving toward me. When I looked up, Canaan was sliding into the seat across from me.

"So you hang out with Teddy Ryan now?" he asked. He sounded angry. There was a sharp, mean edge in his voice.

"Sometimes," I mumbled. My cheeks were starting to burn, and that sickening feeling crept into my stomach.

"We're supposed to hate him," Canaan said. "He's a brat — a jerk."

"He's being nicer to me than you are." I didn't snap or yell. My voice stayed low because I couldn't make it do anything else. I was too nervous. Too upset by the anger in his voice. But I also knew I was right.

"So what? Is he your boyfriend now?"

"No," I said.

"Don't be stupid, Canaan," Andy said, peering over the back of his seat. "Nasty Nola couldn't get a boy-friend — not even Teddy Ryan."

It felt like my face was on fire. I looked at Canaan, expecting him to say something. To tell Andy to shut up. No matter how bad things were between us, he'd still pick me over them — right? He wouldn't let them get away with calling me that.

But Canaan didn't say a word.

"Nasty Nola," Peter snorted. "Oh yeah. But it's more like Fat Nola now. Or wait — what's her real name again?"

"Fionnula," Canaan answered.

It was like he'd just slapped me.

"What kind of name is that?" Peter asked.

"Fat Fionnula," Andy said. "And she's just going to get fatter with those French fries and that shake."

I glared at Canaan. "You're just gonna let them talk to me like that? Let them call me those names?" I whispered.

"Get your new best friend, Teddy Ryan, to stand up for you," Canaan said. "Since he's so much nicer than me and all."

Andy and Peter had started making up a song, repeating "Fat Fionnula" over and over, throwing in a few of those four-letter words in between. I wanted to cry, but I wouldn't let myself. I wouldn't let them see me in tears. That's what they wanted. That'd just make it more fun for them.

"Shut up!" I yelled. At least, I tried to yell. My voice cracked right in the middle, so I didn't sound as tough as I wanted.

"What are you gonna do about it?" Peter asked.

"Careful," Andy said. "She might sit on us. She's so fat, she'd squish us."

"I mean it," I said. "Quit it, or I'll . . . I'll . . ." But I didn't know what I'd do. I'd never had to stand up for myself before. Canaan had always been there to do it for me. But this time, he was one of the people I had to stand up to.

"You'll what?" Canaan asked. "Tell on us? You've always been a tattletale."

"All right, y'all get out of here," Edna said, coming out from behind the counter. "I ain't gonna put up with that kind of behavior. Y'all are being rude and ugly, and I want you out."

"We ain't even ordered!" Peter whined.

"Eat somewhere else," she snapped. "Out!"

With a bunch of growling and grumbling, Peter and Andy hauled themselves out of the booth and stomped through the door. Edna turned to Canaan then.

"And you," she said. "I am disappointed in you, Canaan Swift. I want you out, too."

"Fine." He stood up and started for the door. At the last minute, though, he turned to face me. "And just so you know," he said, "I never wanted to go to your stupid circus. That crap is for babies. You need to grow up."

"Out!" Edna yelled.

And he left.

Edna didn't ask me if I was okay after that. I think

she could tell I wasn't. Instead she just put a hand on my shoulder and asked, "Do you still want that free dessert?"

I shook my head. "No . . . thank you."

"You sure?"

I nodded. "Yeah. I think I just . . . I think I want to go home." I threw out my half-eaten French fries, but Edna wouldn't let me get rid of the shake.

"Take it home," she said. "If you don't want it now, put it in your freezer for later. No point letting it go to waste."

When I got back to the subdivision, I called Mrs. Hooper to check in. She asked if I wanted to come over and hang out with Felicia — "We're grilling hot dogs," she said.

"No thanks. I'm not real hungry."

"All right. But if you change your mind . . ."

I sat in the house for a while, watching TV, drawing in my sketchbook, reading. I couldn't focus on anything. I just kept thinking of Canaan. Of the things he'd said. Teddy was right — he was just like them.

I decided to go for a walk. Mama said walks were good to clear your head, and I figured I'd give it a try. Honestly, it wasn't working real well — everything I saw on my walk down the street reminded me of Canaan or the other Swift boys. And that just made all my thoughts stew more and more. They didn't clear at all.

"Nola," Mr. Briggs called out from his porch. "How are you doing today?"

"Not so good," I admitted. I walked up his driveway and sat down on the front steps beside him. He was whittling on a block of wood, but it looked like he'd just gotten started, so I couldn't tell what it was going to be just yet.

"I'm sorry to hear that," he said. "Does this have something to do with Canaan or his brothers?"

"How'd you know?"

"Oh, it's an easy guess," he said. "You two kids used to be attached at the hip. But I haven't seen y'all together once since the summer started."

"Well, yeah. It's Canaan. He's just . . ." I chewed on my bottom lip. "He's different. He's mean now. He's not my best friend anymore."

Mr. Briggs sighed. "I'm sorry to hear that, Nola. I really am. Unfortunately, he's lost somebody very important to him, and sometimes when that happens — when people lose someone — they change."

"Like my grandma Lucy?" I asked. "I hear she used

to be a real happy person. It's hard to imagine, though. I've always known her as cranky and loud. Mama says she changed after Grandpa died." My stomach churned as I remembered that broken drill I still hadn't told anyone about.

He nodded. "It's a hard thing, losing someone like that."

"I wonder if Mama changed after my daddy died," I said. I never really thought about it before. Mama had always just been Mama to me.

"She might have, in some ways," Mr. Briggs said. "But she's a strong, strong woman, your mother. And she had you to take care of, to get her through."

"Did you ever lose anybody, Mr. Briggs?"

He nodded slowly. "A long, long time ago. I was in love with a woman. But when I returned from the war, she'd married someone else. It broke my heart."

"Wow," I said. "I'm sorry."

"It's all right," he said. "That was a long time ago. And everything happens for a reason. She spent the rest of her life married to Clay Hooper, and she was very happy."

"Wait, Hooper?" I asked. "You were in love with Felicia's grandmother?"

"Her great-grandmother," he said. "And yes, I was. Like I said — everything happens for a reason. If she hadn't married Clay, Felicia wouldn't be here. But losing her was hard. And it did change me — in good ways and bad."

"Do . . . do you think losing Canaan will change me?" I asked. Saying it out loud, that I was losing him, made everything hurt worse. It made it real and opened up a hole in my heart. "Do you think I'll get mean like he and Grandma Lucy did? Or quiet, like Kevin?"

"I think," Mr. Briggs said, pausing between each of his words, "that you are very much like your mama. I think you're stronger than most people your age. . . . And I'm not so sure you've lost Canaan."

"I am," I murmured. "I didn't want to believe it, but after today . . . I don't think we'll ever be the same kinda friends again."

"I hate to hear that," he said. "But, you know, sometimes growing up also means growing apart."

"Maybe I don't want to grow up," I said.

Mr. Briggs kept chipping away at the wooden block, a soft smile settling on his wrinkled face. "None of us do."

# Seven Summers Ago

When we were five, me and Canaan decided to run away. We were two weeks away from starting kindergarten, and neither of us wanted to, so we packed duffel bags with toys, a couple of apples, and my favorite blanket before making our escape.

"We're running away," I announced to Mama as Canaan and I made our way out the front door.

She didn't even glance up from the book she was reading. "All right," she said. "Just don't cross the street by yourselves."

We marched out the front door and headed down the sidewalk together. "Where should we run away to?" I asked Canaan.

"That way," he said, pointing off to the right. "That looks like a good way to run away to."

We'd taken a few steps when Felicia hollered at us from her front yard across the street. "Canaan! Nola! Where y'all going?" She was standing in her driveway, clutching a Barbie doll.

"We're running away," Canaan told her. "So we don't gotta go to kindergarten."

"Can I come?"

"We ain't supposed to cross the street," I told her. "Maybe you can come next time we run away."

"Oh, okay." She looked disappointed, but she went back to playing with her doll, and me and Canaan kept walking, heading down the street with our duffel bag hanging between us.

We walked past a few more houses before we reached Mr. Briggs's front porch. He was sitting on the step, whittling the way he always was. "Morning, Mr. Briggs," Canaan said, waving.

Mr. Briggs looked up from the piece of wood in his hand. "Good morning. Where y'all off to?"

"We're running away," I said.

"So we don't have to go to kindergarten," Canaan explained.

"I see. Where are you running away to?"

"End of the street," Canaan said.

Mr. Briggs nodded. "Well, that's an awful long way to run. Y'all have time to take a rest? I've got lemonade and cookies inside."

"We always got time for cookies," Canaan said. "Right, Nola?"

I nodded.

We followed Mr. Briggs inside and sat down at his kitchen table while he poured us some lemonade. He set a plate of cookies between us and told us to help ourselves.

"So what's this about not wanting to start school?" he asked, easing himself into a wooden chair.

"We ain't going," I said. "Kindergarten sounds hard."

"And boring," Canaan said.

"And scary," I added.

"Don't know about all that," Mr. Briggs said. "You never know. It might be fun. You might like it."

"I don't know," I said.

"And even if it ain't fun," he continued, "y'all got each other, right? Y'all can take care of each other, even if it is hard and scary. Way I see it, if you two can run away together, you can face anything together."

"You think so?" Canaan asked.

"I sure do." Mr. Briggs leaned back in his chair and closed his eyes. "I think school will just be another adventure for the two of you. And I know y'all like adventures."

We finished our cookies and left Mr. Briggs asleep in his chair. We decided we were done with running away for the day. And on the first day of school a couple weeks later, we walked into our classroom, hand in hand, ready for a new adventure.

# Chapter Fourteen

Felicia called me a few days later to ask if I wanted to go to the mall with her that weekend.

"And Teddy Ryan's coming, too," she said. I could hear a giggle in her voice, but I didn't understand why it was there.

"Sounds fun," I said. "Sure. I'd love to come."

I hadn't been to the mall in months. It was in the next county and took thirty minutes to get there. Mama said it wasn't worth the cost of gas when you could get everything you needed at the Walmart in Bunker, which was closer.

Walmart didn't have a Claire's, though. Or a Hot Topic. The mall was obviously better, and I hoped that maybe shopping with Felicia and Teddy would cheer me up a little. Ever since the incident with Canaan at Rocky's, I hadn't been feeling real cheerful.

I got up early Saturday and tried to flat-iron my hair — if I was going to the mall, I wanted to look all right. I even wore a purple sundress Mamaw and Papaw had bought for my birthday. After I put on my sandals, I walked into the living room, where Mama and Richard were talking. They stopped the minute I walked through the door. Just got real quiet.

"What?" I asked, feeling a little nervous. "Is something wrong?"

"Oh no, baby," Mama said. "It's just . . . we were talking about moving plans and I know it's something you don't like to think about —"

"I don't mind," I said.

I could see through the front window, the one that looked out over the duplex's two driveways. I could see Canaan walking out to the street, where Peter and Andy were waiting for him.

"Actually . . . I might be happy to move."

Mama was stunned. "Really?"

I nodded, but I was quick to change the subject. I

didn't want Mama asking questions I was still too hurt to answer. "I better get going. Mrs. Hooper is waiting for us."

"Where you going?" Richard asked.

"The mall."

"Oh, well, in that case. Here," Richard said, pulling out his wallet. "I've got you covered."

"Honey, you don't have to do that," Mama told him.

"Yeah, you don't gotta," I told him. "I've got some extra money from all the jobs I've been working."

"I do have to, actually," he replied. "I still owe you for some help you gave me on the yard a few weeks ago." I was about to remind him that he'd paid me for that a while ago, but then he winked at me, and I knew to keep my mouth shut. "I think this is what I owe you," he said, handing me a twenty-dollar bill.

"Thank you," I said, smiling up at him.

"No problem," he said. "Just remember, be —"

"Frugal?" I offered. "Thrifty? Economical?"

"Wow, I never realized so many of your vocab words were synonyms for cheap," he said. "But yes. You got the point."

I gave them both a hug before heading out the front door. Canaan and his new friends had already gone by the time I started walking to Felicia's house. I ran up the driveway and rang the doorbell. Inside, I could hear JW going wild, barking and growling like a dog five times his size.

"Coming!" Felicia hollered. A second later she pulled open the door, saying, "Back! Back, JW! Hey, Nola. Come on in. I think we're almost ready to go — and Teddy's already here."

JW had stopped barking, but now he was jumping all over my bare legs, leaving a couple little red scratches. I didn't mind, though. I knelt down and scratched behind his floppy puppy ears.

"Hi, Nola," Teddy Ryan said. He was sitting on the sofa, wearing his usual khaki pants and striped shirt.

"Hey."

A second later, Mrs. Hooper walked in the room. She looked real nice in a green dress and heels with her black hair pulled back into a neat bun. She snapped her purse shut and slung it over her shoulder. "All right, kids. Let's head out."

Turns out, Mrs. Hooper had a job interview that afternoon at a law office just a few blocks from the mall.

"Daddy's gonna start working from home so that she can go back to work," Felicia explained to Teddy and me as we made our way through the mall's main entrance.

"Why would she want to do that?" Teddy asked. "Who wants to work if they don't gotta?"

Felicia shrugged. "She said something about needing to be around adults more often. I don't get it, either, but she's real excited. And I think Daddy's looking forward to being at home with JW and me."

We stopped in front of the giant directory and tried to find the little *You Are Here* arrow on the map. This mall wasn't huge compared to the ones I'd seen on TV, but since none of us were here too often, all the departments and store names felt a little intimidating.

"Where do we even start?" I asked.

"I want to go to the bookstore," Felicia said. "Oh, and the candy store. And the pet store — I need to get JW a new food bowl since he chewed his up."

"Maybe we should pick out all the places we want to go," Teddy said, "and then we can try to make a route around the mall that gets us to all of them eventually. That shouldn't be hard since it's just a big square."

So we went down the hallway to the left and made a beeline for the pet store. I held on to my money right up until we got to the crafts store, where I bought a new sketchbook and some nice colored pencils.

"I didn't know you liked to draw," Teddy said.

"She's real good, too," Felicia told him. "She drew me a picture of JW that I put up on my wall."

"Could you draw me something?" Teddy asked.

"Maybe," I said as I handed my twenty-dollar bill to the woman at the register. "I'm not *that* good."

"I bet you are, though," he said. "You don't gotta, but I'd love to have one of your drawings."

I blushed.

The cashier handed me my change — enough to get a slice of cookie cake from the Cookie Palace next door — and we headed out of the craft shop. We'd barely taken a few steps when I heard someone calling after me.

"Nola!"

I looked over my shoulder and my jaw nearly hit the floor. Brian was walking toward me, a big smile on his face. He looked about a million times better than he did last time I saw him. His hair was neat and his clothes were clean, and there was just a warmth about him that I hadn't felt in a long time.

"Hey," he said, reaching out and giving me a quick hug. Then he noticed my friends. "Hi, Felicia. Hi, Teddy."

"What are you doing here?" I asked.

"I came with some of my friends," he said. "Ty and the others are looking at video games right now, but I don't have any money, so . . . Are y'all about to get cookies?"

"Not me," Teddy said, sounding glum. "I'm allergic to the stuff in cookie cake. I tried to sneak some chocolate chips the other day, but they made me break out and Mama noticed." He pointed to a few of the zits on his face.

"Which stuff are you allergic to?" Brian asked. "Like, milk or the chocolate?"

"Yeah, both," Teddy said. "And everything else."

"Come on," I said to Brian. "You can have some of my slice."

I ordered a big slice of chocolate cookie cake, then me and Brian sat down on a bench to split it while Teddy and Felicia headed to the bookstore.

"Where you been?" I asked. "I ain't seen you in a while."

"Oh, you know, just with friends," he said, spearing a piece of cookie cake on his plastic fork. "I've stayed at Ty's place a few times. At Donnie's place, too."

"So you ain't been home?" I asked.

"Just to get more clothes once," he said. "But I haven't been there hardly at all in a couple weeks, I guess. How are my brothers doing?"

I chewed on my bottom lip a second before answering. "It's . . . hard to say. I don't hardly see Canaan no more. And every time I do, he's with Peter and Andy."

Brian made a face. "I thought he hated them."

"I did, too. Guess we were wrong."

"Well . . . What about Kevin? How's he?"

"He's come over for dinner a few times," I said. "But he doesn't say nothing, so I can't really say how well he's doing. . . . You really oughta go home and see them, Brian."

"I know." He looked down at his lap. "I just . . . I needed to get out, Nola. I couldn't take it anymore. Taking care of everything was just too much pressure, you know?"

I nodded, but the truth was, I didn't. I had no idea

what Brian was going through. I couldn't imagine having one of my parents leave without saying good-bye, or the other being so heartbroken she didn't do anything but go to work and go to bed. As much as I wanted Brian to come home and help his brothers — maybe talk to Canaan about what a jerk he was being — I couldn't really blame him for staying gone, neither.

For a second I thought about telling him what I'd found out about his daddy. About the waitress, Sarah Clarke, that he was living with in Bunker. But before I could get the words out of my mouth, Felicia was hurrying out of the bookstore with Teddy behind her, hollering at me.

"We gotta go," she said, grabbing my arm.

"We're supposed to meet Mrs. Hooper at the front entrance at three," Teddy said. He held out his wrist so I could see his bright blue watch. It was 2:57.

"We gotta go," Felicia repeated, tugging on my arm. "Mama will worry if we're late."

"Oh, okay." I stood up, and so did Brian. I gave him one more hug and said, "Hopefully I'll see you soon."

He nodded. "See you later, Nola."

And then I let Felicia pull me away.

# Two Summers Ago

Mr. Swift was taking the boys camping.

I'd been jealous all week, wishing I could go, too. I'd never been camping before. Never even slept in a tent. And normally I went anywhere the boys did, but this time, I hadn't been invited.

"Daddy says it's a men's-only weekend," Kevin told me the day before they left. "We're going down to Kentucky Lake. And we're gonna fish. And we're gonna roast marshmallows and see all sorts of animals. But don't worry, Nola. Daddy says there ain't bears. At least none that'll eat us. So we'll come back and tell you all about it."

But the day they were supposed to leave, Canaan showed up on my front steps, asking if I wanted to go to the playground.

"I thought y'all were going camping," I said.

"Not no more," he said. "Dad left this morning. He and Mama were arguing and he said he needed some space and the trip is off."

"I'm sorry," I said.

"Me too. I was looking forward to camping. Kevin's real upset, though. More than me and Brian are."

Richard was in the living room, sitting on the couch. He stood up and walked over to the doorway where I was talking to Canaan. "Tell you what," he said. "Y'all might not be able to go to Kentucky Lake, but there's no reason you can't camp. Canaan, go tell your brothers to come over here after dinner tonight. And make sure it's okay with your mama if you stay out."

"What are we doing?" Canaan asked.

"We got plenty of backyard," Richard told him. "And I got a tent."

So that night, Richard pitched his old green tent in our backyard. Then we walked down to the woods behind the duplex and found an empty space to light a fire. Richard did that, of course. The only time we were allowed by the fire was when we had marshmallows speared on the end of long sticks.

Richard told us ghost stories, too. And when it got late, he put out the flames and walked us back up to the tent, which was big enough for all four of us to climb in, our sleeping bags side by side.

"I'll be in the house," Richard said. "So will Nola's mama. If y'all need anything, just come get us, all right?"

We all nodded and he smiled before zipping up the tent.

*My sleeping bag was between Canaan's and Kevin's. It didn't take long at all for Canaan and Brian to fall asleep — they both snored, too — but Kevin and I stayed up a little bit longer, whispering.*

*"I really like Richard," Kevin said. "He's real nice. And I'm glad he helped us camp because I was real sad when Daddy said we weren't gonna get to this weekend. And this is better than Kentucky Lake anyhow because you got to camp with us. Nola, do you think your mama is gonna marry Richard?"*

*"I don't know," I said. "I hope so."*

*"Me too," Kevin said. "I want Richard to live next door all the time, not just visit, and I want him to let us camp more. And to make marshmallows. And if he marries your mama, then he'd kind of be your daddy, even though not really. And I think he'd be a nice daddy to have."*

*"I think so, too."*

*Kevin jabbered on and on, and I fell asleep to the sound of his sweet, soft voice.*

# Chapter Fifteen

I was gonna be a junior bridesmaid at Mama and Richard's wedding, which meant I had a lot of responsibilities on my plate. Like on Sunday, when we got up early and headed to a bridal store a few hours away, in Indiana. Mama had already checked out the ones closer to home, but she hadn't found anything she liked. But the store in Indiana was supposed to have all sorts of dresses, so we had high hopes.

"What do you think of this one?" Mama asked, gesturing to one of the wedding dresses on display.

"I like it," I said. But, to be honest, they all looked pretty much the same to me. They were all white, all poufy — what was the difference? I was much more interested in the bridesmaid dresses. At least those were different colors and designs.

"Maybe I'll try it on," she said. "Go ahead and keep looking at the bridesmaid dresses, and I'll go find a salesperson."

I walked around the store, looking at all the mannequins and racks full of hangers. Mama and Richard had already picked their wedding colors, and Mama said the bridesmaids would all be in coral pink. I'd already found a few I really liked, and I was excited to show them to Mama after she'd tried on the wedding dress.

"Nola," I heard her call a few minutes later. "Can you come here?"

I found her poking her head out of a dressing room. She smiled and opened the door a tiny bit so I could squeeze through.

"Can you come help me?" she asked, turning her back toward me and handing me the clips the saleslady had left her with. All the try-on dresses were real big, so you had to clip them in the back to make them look all right.

"Sure." I put the clips in place and stepped back so Mama could turn from side to side to pose in front of the long mirror. "I like it," I told her. "You look real pretty."

"Thank you, baby," she said. But then she sighed. "I don't know, though. I don't think it's *the one*. I'm starting to get stressed about this. We really didn't leave much time to plan the wedding — and we only have four weeks left."

"So y'all picked a date?" I asked.

"Yep. Just yesterday — August eighth. We already booked the church."

I felt a lump rise up into my throat. It felt like I'd swallowed a Ping-Pong ball. "August eighth?" I repeated.

Mama nodded, still facing the mirror and smoothing her hands down the dress.

"The day of the circus."

In a lot of places, the circus would stick around for a whole weekend. But not in little old Besser County. We were lucky for the traveling to circus to come every five years, and they never stayed more than one day.

"Oh." Mama turned to face me, her hand covering

her mouth. "Oh, baby, I forgot that was the same day. I'm really sorry."

I shook my head. "It's okay," I said, even though I felt like crying. Deep down, I knew the boys and I probably wouldn't go to the circus like we'd planned for so long. But I'd held on to this little shred of hope. This idea that maybe, somehow, everything would work out. Mr. Swift would come back, Brian would come home, Kevin would talk again, and Canaan would be Canaan again. Then we'd go to the circus, just like we had a few years ago, and it would be just as fun as it was then, even if we were a little too old for it.

But if the wedding was on August eighth, that meant there was no chance I'd be going to the circus with the boys. That little bit of hope was gone.

And it hurt.

It hurt more than it should have. More than just finding out I wasn't going to the circus. It felt like I was losing something. Not just the boys — something bigger. This was my last summer living next door to the Swifts, and everything had fallen apart. The one thing I'd held on to was gone.

"I'm sorry," Mama said again, reaching out to stroke my hair. "That's the only day we could get in August —"

"It's fine." But my voice broke. I cleared my throat. "It's fine. I'm too old for the circus, anyway."

But I could tell she still felt bad. After she tried on a few more wedding dresses and had me try a couple of coral-pink bridesmaid dresses, we left the store empty-handed and drove back to Kentucky. Once we got back into town, she drove to Rocky's and bought both of us ice cream sundaes.

"What are you gonna do about dresses?" I asked, picking at my ice cream with a plastic spoon. To be honest, I wasn't very hungry, but it would've been rude and wasteful not to eat it.

"A friend of mine from work bought her dress at a store in Nashville. I'll see if I can get a day off this week to go down and look. You can come with me, if you want. We can go eat at the Rainforest Cafe afterwards."

I nodded. "Okay."

Mama opened her mouth, like she was gonna say something else, but then her cell phone buzzed. She pulled it out of her purse and fiddled with the buttons for a second before looking up at me again. "Richard and I have a surprise for you, if you're up for it."

"Sure," I said.

"He just got off work, and we're meeting him there."

"Where?"

"You'll see."

We finished our sundaes and said good-bye to Edna before climbing back into the car. Then Mama started driving down the highway, right into a sunset so bright I had to put a hand over my eyes. We drove out into the country, where you only saw a house every mile or so. Finally, Mama turned off the road and headed up a long gravel driveway.

A minute later we were parked next to Richard's truck, and I was staring up at a brick house. It wasn't real big, just one floor — but it was definitely bigger than the duplex — the whole duplex, not just our side. The yard was full of trees, and I could see the edge of a lake way out in the backyard.

"Where are we?" I asked, even though I thought I knew.

"This is going to be our house," Mama said. "We made an offer last week, and the owners accepted. We can move in next month — right after the wedding."

I stared at the house: at the black shutters on the windows, at the porch swing, at the little chimney on the roof — which meant there must be a fireplace inside.

"Come on," Mama said, opening her door. "We can go in so you can see all of it."

The inside was just as nice — maybe nicer — than the outside. The floor was all hardwood, and the walls had just been painted white. There wasn't any furniture, so the whole place felt really big and open. Especially the living room. There were lots of windows looking out of the yard and, like I'd expected, there was a fireplace in the far corner.

"What do you think, kiddo?" Richard asked, walking out of the kitchen with a big smile on his face.

"It's real nice," I said. And I meant it. The house was beautiful — just like the houses families lived in on TV.

"Your room is this way," Mama said, taking me by the hand and leading me down the hallway. "You have the best view."

My new room was almost twice the size of the one I slept in now. It even had a walk-in closet. But the best part was the window that looked out over the backyard. I could see the lake and hills behind it. And beyond that were thick woods. The window was facing west, so I had the perfect view of the sunset.

"Isn't it great?" Mama said.

"Yeah," I said. "It's beautiful. . . . Can we afford this place, Mama?"

She laughed. "Well, we've been saving for a while. And we got a pretty good deal, so . . . yeah. We can."

"Wow," I murmured.

"Also, Richard and I have been talking," she said, glancing over her shoulder to where Richard stood, leaning against the door frame. "We were thinking . . ."

"Once we get moved in," Richard said, "how would you feel about getting a dog?"

"R-really?" I stammered.

"You've wanted one for years," Mama said. "But we didn't have space. Now we do."

"Can we get a husky?" I asked. "Or a pug? Or both?"

Mama and Richard both laughed. "We'll see," Mama said. "Let's go take a walk outside before it gets too dark."

The new house really was perfect, and the more Mama and Richard talked about their plans, the more excited I got about moving here. About my room, the lake, a dog — it was amazing. Except one thing.

While we walked around the big yard, I couldn't help but notice that there weren't any houses close by. Which meant no neighbors. No kids my age living next door. No more Felicia and Teddy.

No Swift brothers.

In just a few weeks, I'd be leaving the boys. Sure, we'd still see each other at school, but it wouldn't be the same. And just then, looking up at the house with Mama and Richard, I realized that I couldn't leave the boys like that. I'd be miserable knowing I'd abandoned them when they were still so hurt. I had to fix things before I left.

I had to make Mr. Swift come home.

\* \* \*

I walked over to Teddy Ryan's the next day, and for the first time in my life, I actually rang his doorbell.

Mrs. Ryan answered. She was dressed in shorts and a loose T-shirt, her black hair was pulled back, and there was a slight glisten on her skin, like she was sweating.

"Oh, hello, Nola," she panted. "Sorry. I was just getting a workout in. Come on in. Teddy's in his room."

I'd never been inside the Ryans' house before. It was very neat, so clean it almost made me uncomfortable. Like I was afraid I'd mess something up just by touching it. There wasn't a TV in the living room. Just sofas, a few bookshelves, and a nice stereo system.

"Just down the hall," Mrs. Ryan said. "If y'all need anything, I'll be in the spare room."

"Thanks, Mrs. Ryan."

Teddy's door was open. He was sitting on his bed, reading a beat-up paperback of *Harry Potter and the Chamber of Secrets*. He didn't even hear me walk in the room, so after a second, I cleared my throat real loud. He jumped and looked up, big hazel eyes staring at me through thick glasses.

"N-Nola," he stammered. "Hi."

"Hey," I said. "Sorry. I wasn't trying to scare you."

"That's okay," he said, sticking a bookmark between the pages of his book. "What are you doing here?"

"Nothing," I said. "I just, um . . . I need to go to the library, and I wondered if you wanted to come with me?"

He nodded. "I'd love to, but I'm not allowed to ride my bike outside of the subdivision."

"Oh, uh . . . can your mama take us?" I asked. "Or would that be too rude to ask? I know she's exercising right now —"

"She loves the library," Teddy said. "As soon as she's off the treadmill, I'm sure she'll drive us."

"Oh, good."

There was a long pause where I just stood in the middle of Teddy Ryan's bedroom, staring at all his family pictures and posters and trophies. Not a single one of them was related to sports. They were from things like spelling bees and math competitions. I was a grade ahead of Teddy, so I hadn't realized just how smart he was until then.

"I don't like treadmills."

I turned to look at him, surprised. What on earth was he talking about?

He adjusted his glasses. "I don't like treadmills," he said again. "They kind of freak me out. I'm always afraid they'll go too fast and I'll fly off the back."

I laughed. "That sounds like something that'd happen in a cartoon."

"I'm not allowed to watch cartoons," he said. "My parents say they rot your brain."

I didn't know if I should be offended by that or not, since I watched cartoons. But I decided to let it go. Anyway, if I was too old for the circus, I was probably too old for cartoons, too.

"You can sit down," Teddy said, patting the foot of his bed. "You don't gotta stand up. . . . And I can get you a book or something to read if you want."

"That's okay," I told him.

"What do you gotta go to the library for?" he asked.

"I need to use the computers," I said. "And Felicia told me I oughta read *The Hobbit*, so I thought I'd check it out today."

"I haven't read that one yet," Teddy said. "Tell me how you like it, okay?"

"I will."

"You've read the Harry Potter books, though, right?" he asked.

"Of course!" I said. "They're some of my favorites."

So we talked about books for a while; Teddy even showed me a few signed novels his aunt in Atlanta had sent him. He was looking for a book on his shelf when we heard the shower start in the next room.

"That means she's done running," Teddy said.

Half an hour later, Mrs. Ryan was driving us up to the local library. She picked up a magazine and went to sit in a comfy armchair while me and Teddy headed to the computers.

As soon as the Internet had loaded, I started searching for Sarah Clarke. There were lots of Sarah Clarkes, but a few more minutes on Google and I'd tracked down the right woman's address in Bunker. I scribbled it down on a piece of scrap paper and shoved it in my pocket. I was surprised how easy it was to find her address online. A little bit scared, too. Mama was always warning me about the Internet and not putting personal information on here. But I bet if I Googled our names, our address would show up, too.

I still hadn't figured out how I'd get to Bunker to see Mr. Swift, though. Not without visiting Grandma Lucy, which I really didn't want to do. I'd never told her about the broken drill, and I didn't want to be there when she found out. I felt guilty for not telling her, but I was too scared. So I'd need to think of another way to get over to Bunker. And soon.

I leaned over and took a peek at Teddy's screen. He was playing some sort of game where he had to use a gun to pop balloons. When he caught me watching, he shut it down real quick and looked embarrassed.

"Don't tell my mom," he whispered.

"Why not?" I asked.

"I'm not allowed to play video games."

Poor Teddy Ryan. He couldn't eat cake or cookies, he didn't have a TV, and he wasn't allowed to play video games. Thank goodness he had a trampoline, or else I didn't know what he'd do.

Even though I had what I'd come for, I wasn't quite ready to go home or stop hanging out with Teddy yet, so we sat down at a table and started putting together one of the thousand-piece puzzles they kept in the back of the library. It was fun, actually, just talking with Teddy. The puzzle was of a sea lion, and Teddy had just read a book about sea lions, so he told me all about them.

"I'd love to see one in real life," I said.

"You've never seen one at the zoo?" he asked.

I shook my head. "Never been to the zoo. Except the petting zoo on the Kingsleys' farm, but I'm not sure that counts since it's just a couple of goats and sheep. I've been to the circus, though."

"We go to the zoo almost every year," Teddy said. "We can take you this year, if you want. I'm sure my parents won't mind."

"I'd love that," I said, feeling happy at the thought of me and Teddy hanging out even after I moved. "Are there penguins there? I've always wanted to see a penguin up close."

"Oh yeah," he said. "There are penguins. And tigers. The tigers are my favorite."

Mrs. Ryan came over when we were about halfway through the puzzle to tell us it was time to get going. The library closed at five, and Mr. Ryan would be home soon.

She dropped me off in front of the duplex and told me to come visit anytime I wanted. I waved good-bye to her and Teddy before heading inside. Sarah Clarke's address felt like a ten-pound weight in my back pocket. I knew where she lived. Where Mr. Swift lived. I just had to figure out what I'd do next.

# Chapter Sixteen

Mama let me invite Felicia down to Nashville with us and promised to take us to the Rainforest Cafe after we went to the bridal shop. While Mama tried on wedding dresses, Felicia and I hunted through the racks, picking out our favorite gowns.

"I *love* this one," Felicia said, holding up a long purple dress with puffy sleeves. "I'd look like a princess in this, don't you think?"

I nodded. "It's pretty," I said, even though I kinda didn't like it.

"Can you draw a picture of me in a dress like this?" she asked.

"I don't know . . . maybe." I felt myself blush and

looked away. I liked to draw, and I even thought some of the things I did were pretty good, but when other people mentioned my drawings or said nice things about them, I got embarrassed.

"You're so good at drawing, I bet you could. You should draw something for Teddy, too. I know he'd like that." She put the dress back on the rack. "He told me y'all went to the library."

"Yep. I checked out *The Hobbit*, just like you told me to."

"Good. You'll love it."

"Maybe when I finish it, we can have a slumber party and talk about it or something?" I suggested.

"That'd be fun!" she said, clapping her hands together. But then, she suddenly got real serious. "Nola, can I ask you something?"

"Sure." But the way she said it made my stomach flip-flop.

Felicia took a deep breath. "Are you only hanging out with me and Teddy because Canaan and his brothers aren't around much now?" She tugged on one of her braids. "I mean, I know they were your best friends, but I've always been your friend, too. And, I don't know, I always felt like you didn't like me as much as them. I felt left out. And now all of a sudden we're spending a lot more time together — and you're spending time with Teddy, too — and I can't help feeling like it's because you ain't got no one else to be friends with."

Even though Felicia was being real sweet and quiet and nice, I felt like I was in trouble. Like I'd done something wrong. My belly wobbled and my eyes started to sting with tears. I took a few deep breaths and tried to pull myself together.

The truth was, when I first started spending more time with Felicia, it had been because I needed a friend. But over the summer, I'd gotten a lot closer to her. And to Teddy. And I felt bad that she'd been left out for all these years.

I thought about how many times we'd forgotten to invite Felicia over to play, or how many times Canaan had chased off Teddy when he tried to talk to me. We never meant no harm, but maybe being so close to the boys for so long had kept me from making other friends.

Since Felicia was brave enough to be honest with me, I decided to be honest with her, too. I hoped she'd take it okay.

"At first, maybe it was because the boys weren't around," I admitted. "But not anymore. I really have fun with you and with Teddy. And even if the boys were back to normal, I'd still want to spend time with you and Teddy like I have been. I mean it. Y'all are my friends."

She smiled. "Okay. Good. I just wanted to make sure." Her smile turned to a grin. "And I *know* Teddy would be happy to hear it."

"What do you mean?"

"Nothing," she said with a giggle. "It's a secret. I can't tell."

"Can't tell what?"

"*Nothing*," she repeated. Then she picked up another dress — a strapless lavender one. "This one would look real pretty on you, Nola. When you draw me in the purple dress, draw you next to me in this one, okay?"

✳ ✳ ✳

Mama found her perfect wedding dress that day, and she ordered my junior bridesmaid dress online. So we spent the rest of the week mailing invitations and picking out the flower arrangements. The wedding was coming up fast, and Mama was pretty much always in a state of panic these days. And when Mama was stressed, so was I.

But what was stressing me out most was Grandma Lucy. She'd called and asked Mama if I'd mind helping her clean up the house that weekend. I wanted to say no. The idea of seeing Grandma Lucy again, of maybe getting in trouble for breaking Grandpa's drill, terrified me. But I was so, so close to finding Mr. Swift. I had his address and everything. And even though I'd been trying to think of another way to get to Bunker, visiting Grandma Lucy seemed like my only choice. So I had to suck it up and hope, hope, hope she hadn't and wouldn't notice the drill.

Mama and Richard dropped me and my bike off on their way to look at tuxes. Grandma Lucy opened the front door for me and waved me inside without a word.

"I'll get started right away," I told her, hoping that if I was working, I wouldn't have to talk to her much. I was sure that the more time we spent together, the more obvious it would be that I'd done something wrong. "Do you already have the cleaning supplies? Like glass cleaner for the windows? If not, I can go get them from the store. I brought my bike again."

"Don't you be worrying about that. You're not cleaning nothing."

"I'm not?"

"Not today," Grandma Lucy said as she led the way toward the kitchen. I followed along behind her, feeling awfully confused and even more nervous. She picked up the keys she'd left on the counter — the keys to the garage.

"So, what're we doing, then?" I asked, trying not to panic. What if she'd seen the drill? What if she'd just asked me to come over here so she could yell at me?

"Making your mama a wedding gift. Come on." She headed back down the hallway and through the front door. I dragged my feet, wishing I could just disappear. Once we were outside, she opened the small side door of the garage and hollered for me to follow her inside. "Which of these boxes did you put all the pictures in?"

"Um . . ." I looked at the boxes, trying to remember. But I was too focused on trying to hide the workbench, standing with my back to it so she couldn't see the broken drill, still in the spot I'd left it.

"You don't know?" Grandma Lucy asked. "What

was the point of me paying you to clean up out here if you don't even know where you put things?"

My stomach knotted up, and I started to feel like I might start crying. I swallowed, hard, then pointed to one of the large boxes. "Th-that one, I think."

"All right. Then help me carry it inside."

That's when I started to panic for a different reason. I'd been counting on a trip to the store for supplies — that was my chance to go to Sarah Clarke's house and talk to Mr. Swift about going back home. If Grandma Lucy was going to keep me busy inside, with her, I'd never be able to sneak away.

We sat down on the couch and opened the box together. Grandma Lucy pulled out the dusty photo album, and for a minute she just held it in her lap, staring down at the plain black cover. I thought she might cry — she had that sort of sparkle in her eye — but she just cleared her throat, shoved the album at me, and said, "Stay right there. I'll be back."

She headed down the hallway, and I heard a few cabinets and drawers slam in the kitchen. When she came back, she was carrying a piece of square cardboard, a picture frame, and some glue. She sat down next to me and dumped all the stuff on the coffee table.

"What're we doing?" I asked again, fidgeting in my seat.

"It oughta be obvious, Fionnula," she said. "Haven't you seen a collage before?"

I had, of course. We'd made lots of them in elementary school. I'd just never expected to be making one with her.

She began pulling out pictures — one by one — picking out the ones she wanted to put in Mama's wedding collage. They were all pictures from a long time ago — ones of Mama as a kid, ones of her with my grandpa. Each time Grandma Lucy pulled out one of those, she gave a sad smile.

"You sure you wanna use those?" I asked, feeling even guiltier about Grandpa's drill, knowing how much all his stuff meant to her. "You don't got any copies. Don't you wanna keep them for yourself?"

She shook her head. "I've been able to look at these for many years." For once, her voice was soft. Not harsh or cranky. "Your mother should have them now."

We spent about an hour spreading glue on the back of photos and arranging them on the piece of cardboard.

When we were done, Grandma Lucy fitted it into the frame she'd brought out.

"Fionnula," she said, not looking at me. "You know, you can come see me anytime. You don't have to be working. You can just visit."

I hadn't expected her to say anything like that. But I suppose I shouldn't have been surprised. Last time I'd seen her, she'd apologized for all the yelling she did. I guess I'd always thought Grandma Lucy didn't really like me too much, but maybe I was wrong.

"It's been real nice seeing you more often lately," Grandma Lucy said. "I just wish we'd gotten to visit more, I suppose." She finished with the picture frame and held up the collage for me to see. "How's it look?"

"Mama will love it," I said.

"Good," she said. "It can be from both of us."

She made sandwiches for us and we sat on the couch, eating and watching black-and-white movies on some cable channel Mama and I didn't have. I was getting antsy — I didn't know how long it would be before Mama and Richard came to pick me up, and I still needed to go find Mr. Swift.

I got my chance about half an hour later when

Grandma Lucy nodded off on the sofa. Once she started snoring like a freight train, I hopped up and headed out the front door. Sarah Clarke's address was in my back pocket, and I was pretty sure I knew how to get there, too. But I had to be fast.

I rode toward town and made a right at the stoplight just past the Country Kitchen. Sarah Clarke lived in an apartment complex Mama and I had passed a few times on our way to Grandma Lucy's house. It took me a minute to find the right door, she lived in 1D, but eventually I found it.

I was stashing my bike in the bushes when I heard the apartment door open. I ducked down, not sure why, but feeling like I oughta be hiding. Sarah walked out, dressed in her pink waitress uniform, and Mr. Swift was behind her. It was the first time I'd gotten a good look at him since the night he'd left.

And he looked all right — like he'd gotten a haircut, maybe, and his clothes looked ironed and neat. He looked a lot better than his boys had looked lately, and something about seeing that made my fists clench into balls.

"Have a nice day," he said, giving her a kiss. Right on the mouth, too. "I love you."

I knew she'd said they might get married, but something about seeing him kiss her, hearing him say he loved her, made it so much more real. So much worse.

Sarah waved good-bye and went out to the parking lot. Mr. Swift watched her walk away, then he turned and went back inside. Now was my chance. Now was the time to go knock on the door and do what I'd come to do.

But I couldn't.

I'd made it all this way, done all this work to track him down, and I couldn't move. I was too scared to knock on his door. Too scared to confront him. And, all of a sudden, it didn't really feel like it was my business, no matter how much I wanted to help the boys.

Feeling sick and ashamed and cowardly, I pulled my bike back out of the bushes. I pedaled hard all the way back to Grandma Lucy's house. I was so upset — mad at Mr. Swift and at myself — that I didn't even think about how I'd left my grandmother asleep on the couch without letting her know where I was going. But as soon as I dropped my bike on the front porch, the front door flew open and she came storming out.

By the look on her face, I knew she was mad. At first I thought maybe she'd seen the drill, found out I'd been keeping it from her. That was something else I was being a chicken about. But then she started yelling.

"Fionnula Sutton, I could tan your hide right now!" Her voice was loud and screechy. "I was worried sick — I almost called the police when I woke up and saw you weren't there. Where were you? What in the Lord's name were you thinking?"

I didn't say anything. It was all too much just then. I buried my face in my hands and just started bawling. Because I felt guilty about the drill. Because I was in trouble for going into town. Because I'd chickened out at the last minute. Because Mr. Swift was in love with Sarah Clarke and I didn't know if he'd ever go back home. Because the wedding was coming up and I'd be moving and everything was a mess.

"Fionnula?" Grandma Lucy asked. "What is it? What's the matter?"

I was crying too hard to answer. So I just shook my head. After a second, Grandma Lucy walked toward me and put her arms around me.

"Shhh," she said. "Shh. It's all right. It's gonna be all right."

But I wasn't so sure it would.

# Four Summers Ago

I wanted to crawl into a hole and never come out that day. Or maybe vanish into the woods and never come back. I thought I was being nice when I picked a handful of flowers from Miss Shirley's garden and made a bouquet for Mama, but the minute she'd seen them her face had turned red and she'd started scolding me.

"Those are Miss Shirley's flowers," she'd said. "You can't just go picking them. She works hard on those. You have to go apologize. Now."

The boys were outside when I headed up the driveway. Kevin — he was only four — pointed and asked, "Why's Nola crying? Is she sad? Is she hurt? What's wrong with her?"

I told the boys what I had to do, and Canaan said he'd come with me to Miss Shirley's. "It'll be okay," he said. "She's so nice. She won't get mad. And her vision ain't good, you know, so even if she tries to, like, hit you, she'll probably miss."

But when we got to her front porch, I just stood there, feeling panicked. I couldn't knock on her door and tell her what I'd done. I couldn't. I just couldn't. Seeing how scared I was, Canaan hopped up the steps and knocked himself.

"Canaan!" I hissed.

But when Miss Shirley answered, he was the one that did all the talking. "Hi, ma'am," he said. "I came here to apologize. I picked some of your flowers for my mama today, and I didn't know that was wrong, but she told me, and I'm real sorry about it. Real sorry, ma'am."

Miss Shirley wasn't mad at all. She said it was an honest mistake and offered me and Canaan some tea.

"I feel bad you did that," I told him on our way back to the duplex.

"Why? She wasn't mad."

"I know, but I'm the one who did it. I shouldn't have chickened out. You can't always help me when I get too scared."

"Sure I can," Canaan said. "You're my best friend, so I'll always be around to help if you chicken out. Just as long as you'll be around if I need help, like, running from bears or climbing a mountain or something."

"There ain't no bears around here," I said. "Or mountains. And I wouldn't be no good at that stuff, anyway."

"But I'm gonna go places where there are bears and mountains one day," he said. "And you're coming, too, and I'll teach you how to be good at it. You're not good at basketball, either, but we always win as a team, don't we?"

"Most of the time."

"Exactly," he said. "So that's when you can help me out. And until then, it's okay if you chicken out. Deal?"

It didn't seem all that fair. Even in his plans for the future, he had to help me learn to help him. But he didn't mind, and I liked the idea of climbing mountains with him one day. So I just laughed. "All right. Deal."

# Chapter Seventeen

Mama could tell I was depressed. She kept offering to buy me milkshakes that week or to take me to the movies, but I always said no. All I really wanted to do was sit in my room, draw pictures, and "mope." That's what Richard said I was doing, at least.

"What's the matter?" Mama asked me one morning before she left for work. "I don't think you've left the house in days."

I shrugged and kept eating my Cheerios.

"Oh no." Mama sighed. "Is this some sort of teenage hormone thing? Because I don't know if I'm ready for that yet."

"I'm not a teenager," I told her.

"It won't be long before you are, though," she said.

I shrugged again.

"Grandma Lucy said something that really got you upset last Saturday." She touched my shoulder. "What's going on, Nola Baby? You can tell me."

I could've, but I didn't want to. First off, I'd be in trouble for doing all that hunting for Mr. Swift. But also, it was just too hard to say it out loud. To say I couldn't bring him back like I wanted to and the boys were just gonna have to keep being hurt. That I was leaving them that way, just like he had.

And, to be honest, I hadn't talked to Mama much about the Swift boys because I didn't want to burden her when she was so busy with the wedding and the move and everything.

"I'm fine," I lied.

Mama let out another sigh, ran her hand through my curly hair, and kissed me on the cheek. "Promise me you'll leave the house while I'm at work," she said. "Go visit Felicia. Or Teddy."

"All right."

"You promise?"

"I promise."

"Good. I love you. I'll see you tonight."

"Bye, Mama."

I watched TV on the couch for a while, flipping through the channels every five minutes because nothing good was on. It was about three o'clock when the phone rang.

"Hello?" I said into the receiver. I figured it was Mrs. Hooper calling to check in on me. But instead, it was Felicia.

"Nola." Her voice was choked, like she was crying. "Have you seen JW anywhere?"

"No. I ain't been outside. Why? You can't find him?"

"Uh-uh," she said. "I let him out into the backyard, but he ain't there anymore. I've looked all over for him. Can you help me?"

"Of course. I'll go out and holler for him now."

"Thank you."

I put on my sandals and headed outside. It was hot, and there wasn't a cloud in the sky. I could already feel the sunburn sizzling across my skin.

"Jabberwocky!" I yelled, walking down my driveway, toward the street. "JW! Jabberwocky! Here, boy!"

I made a loop around the subdivision, hollering for him over and over and letting everyone I passed know to keep an eye out for a little yellow dog. I was starting to get worried. JW wasn't real big yet. If another dog picked a fight with him, he was a goner. I didn't even like to think about it.

I'd just rounded the corner and was on my way back toward the duplex when I heard yelping sounds. A second later, I saw something that made me feel sick. Canaan, Andy, and Peter — all of them were on the sidewalk ahead, and there was JW, a fat little thing at their feet, barking and crying, trying to get away as they kicked and pulled at him.

And laughed.

Andy had a foot on JW's tail so he couldn't get away. "Stupid dog," he was saying to the other boys. "And ugly, too."

"Just like its owner," Peter said. "I can't stand Felicia."

"What should we do with him?" Andy asked while Peter bent down to yank on JW's ear so hard the puppy yelped.

I decided I didn't want to hear the answer to that.

"Hey!" I screamed, gathering up every bit of courage I had. "Leave the dog alone!"

All three of the boys looked over at me. Both Andy and Peter smiled wickedly, but Canaan didn't. I couldn't tell what he was thinking. Or feeling. His face was blank as paper.

"Fat Fionnula," Andy said. "What do you want?"

"Give me the puppy," I told him. "You're hurting him."

"What do you care?" Peter asked. "Ain't your puppy."

"It's my friend's dog," I said. "And even if he wasn't, I still wouldn't let you hurt him. Now get off his tail."

"Mind your own business," Andy said.

"This *is* my business," I said. "Felicia asked me to find her dog, and I did. Now let me have him."

"All right," Andy said. There was a grin on his face that made me nervous. "You can have him. Take him."

He lifted his foot, freeing JW's tail. I knelt down and scooped the dog into my arms. He was getting awful heavy, and it took me a second to get my balance. Before I could stand up, though, something hard hit me in the side and sent me and JW down onto the sidewalk.

"Fat Fionnula," Andy said, leering down at me. He'd

been the one to kick me just then. "I bet you're like a turtle. Bet you can't get up once you're down."

Peter laughed, like that was the funniest thing he'd ever heard.

I squeezed JW tight. He barked and growled at the boys, squirming in my arms as I tried to get back up. I was just about to when Andy kicked me again. Not so hard that it hurt real bad, but hard enough to keep me down.

"Told you," Andy said. "Just like a turtle. A fat turtle."

I was trying hard not to cry, knowing that would mean they'd won. But I didn't know how I'd get out of here. There were three of them and just one of me, and right now they wouldn't even let me get on my feet. Part of me was scared, but part of me was angry, too. Angry at Peter, Andy, and Canaan for being such jerks. And angry at myself for not being strong enough or brave enough to fight back.

"Leave her alone."

I looked up and was shocked to see Canaan. He was standing with his back to me, blocking me from the other boys.

"What do you care?" Peter asked. "You ain't friends with her no more. It's just Nasty Nola."

"Fat Fionnula," Andy corrected.

"Shut up," Canaan said. "And back off her."

I was so surprised that Canaan was standing up for me that I didn't even know how to feel. Part of me was happy — because this was something the old Canaan would do. Part of me was mad he'd let it get this far before saying something. And another part of me was disappointed I still needed his help. But mostly, I was just relieved the other two had stopped kicking me, and I really wanted to get JW out of there before they noticed us again.

"Make me," Andy said.

Everything happened fast after that, and I didn't stick around long enough to try and make sense of it. I got to my feet, JW in my arms, and took off toward Felicia's as fast as I could. But from what I saw, Canaan threw the first punch.

# Chapter Eighteen

Felicia was awful glad to see JW again. She hugged the dog close while he wiggled and licked at her face. "Thank you," she said. "I was so worried about him."

"I'm glad I found him." I didn't tell her how I'd found him. Or where. Or who with. That'd just make her as upset as I was, and I didn't want to do that. Besides, JW seemed fine. Like he'd already forgotten what the boys had been doing to him. I wish I could have.

"You wanna come inside?" she asked. "Daddy made a cake to celebrate. Mama got that job she interviewed for."

"No thanks," I said. "Tell her congratulations for me, though."

"All right," she said. "I will. See you later, Nola."

I was a little dazed on my walk across the street. I couldn't believe what had just happened. I couldn't believe Canaan had stood up for me. What did it mean? Was he done being mad at me? Or was he just sick of Andy and Peter? I wondered how bad the fight had gotten and if he was all right.

I was in for another shock when I got back to the duplex. Brian was there, sitting on the Swifts' front porch. It was the first time I'd seen him in the neighborhood in weeks.

"Hey," I said, walking across the patch of grass between our driveways. "You're home."

He nodded. "Yeah . . . I couldn't stay gone forever."

"You say that like it's a bad thing," I said.

"It might be."

Neither of us said anything for a minute. Brian ran a hand through his hair and adjusted his glasses. A few more seconds passed, then he cleared his throat.

"You seen Canaan?"

I nodded. "Yeah . . . He got in a fight with Andy and Peter a little bit ago. I ain't seen him since, though. I'm hoping he's all right."

"I hope so, too."

"Where's Kevin?" I asked.

"Inside taking a nap."

"Isn't your mama at work? And you just got back?"

He nodded.

"So Kevin's been inside by himself all day?"

"I guess so."

The thought of Kevin, quiet and lonely inside his house, broke my heart. Whether he talked or not, Kevin was a social person. He liked people. He didn't like being by himself. It made me sad, but also angry at Mrs. Swift and Canaan and Brian for leaving him alone. Hadn't there been enough leaving already?

Just then I remembered my failed plan to see Mr. Swift, and Sarah Clarke's address, still tucked away in my room. I didn't wanna talk about it or think about it, but I knew the boys deserved to know where their daddy had gone.

"Brian," I said, sitting on the step beside him. "I . . . I was gonna find your daddy. To tell him to come back. I chickened out last minute, thought maybe it wasn't my business, but I did get his address if you want it. He's living in Bunker now with a waitress named —"

"Sarah," Brian said.

I stared at him, surprised. "How'd you know?"

"I found him," he said. "Earlier this summer. I went and saw him."

"So you talked to him? What did he say? What'd you find out?"

"That he's a jerk. That he's not coming back. That he left my mom to be with someone else. That he ain't the father I thought he was." He looked down at his lap, and I thought he might cry like he had that day in the back-yard earlier this summer.

I put my hand over his and squeezed. "I'm sorry," I said.

"You're not the one that oughta be apologizing. He is," Brian said.

"So do . . . do the others know? Canaan and Kevin and your mama? Did you tell them?"

Brian shook his head. "No. And I'm not gonna."

"What? Why not?"

"It'd just hurt them."

"They deserve to know, though," I argued. "Especially Canaan."

Brian shook his head. "I kept it from him for a rea-son, Nola. I hate my dad. I was mad at him for going, but after I found him, I realized I *hated* him. I hate him."

"You don't —"

"I do," he said. "You know why Kevin stopped talking? It's because the night Dad left, he was real irritated with something. Maybe Mama — they'd been fighting again. Or maybe it was something else. I don't know. But Kevin was talking, just chattering away the way he used to. Dad turned to look at him and just snapped. Told him to shut up. Told him he talked too much. Told him he was driving everyone crazy. Ten minutes later, he walked out the door and never came back."

"But he didn't leave because of Kevin," I said.

"We've all told Kevin that," Brian said. "But it hasn't helped. And you know what Dad said when I told him all of that? That Kevin ain't talked since he left? He just shrugged and said Kevin had always been too sensitive. That was it. He didn't even care, Nola. His own kid's gone mute because he thinks he drove his dad away, and the jerk doesn't even care at all. What kind of dad is that?"

"I'm sorry," I said.

"I hate him," Brian repeated. "And I wish I didn't, but I do. I don't want Canaan and Kevin to hate him, too."

"But they oughta know the truth," I said.

"Why?" Brian asked. "They're hurt enough as it is. That'd just hurt them more. It hurt *me* more."

I was about to argue — to remind him that the truth was always the best way — but before I could say anything, I spotted Canaan out of the corner of my eye. He was down the street, headed our way. When he got closer, I saw he had a bloody lip. Brian and I both stood up at once.

"Canaan!" I hollered, running to meet him at the end of the driveway. "You all right? They hurt you bad?"

"I'm fine," he said. "Nola, I'm sorry. About what they did you back there. I knew they were mean, but I never thought they'd knock a girl down."

Before I could say anything, Brian had come up to us. "Come on," he said, taking Canaan by the shoulder. "I'll get you an ice pack."

I started to follow them inside, but Brian stopped me at the door.

"I think I need to be alone with my brothers," he said. Suddenly, he seemed so much older. He'd always seemed old for his age, but just then, something about the look on his face made him seem real old. Like an adult. "We need to talk about stuff — about changes."

"Changes?" I asked.

Brian nodded. "We can't keep things up the way they are," he said. "There's a lot we gotta talk about. Then I gotta talk to my mom tonight. We have to start making things work again. Even if it's tough."

I nodded. "Good luck," I said. "If y'all need anything, me and Mama are just next door. Well, for now. The move is real soon, but . . ."

"Thanks, Nola," Brian said. "You're a good friend."

I stayed there until the door had shut, then I walked back around to my front door and headed inside. I didn't really know what to do with myself. I was full of thoughts and feelings with nowhere to put them. I couldn't sit still. I couldn't focus on anything, not even drawing. Lucky for me, I didn't have to for long. Just a few minutes later, there was a knock on the door.

Teddy Ryan was standing on my front porch, dressed in his usual khakis and striped T-shirt. He gave me a big grin when I opened the door.

"Hey, Nola," he said. "Wanna come jump on my trampoline for a while?"

I nodded. I needed something to do — anything to keep me from thinking about the boys and Mr. Swift. I followed Teddy down the street and we went through his front door, through the kitchen, then out the back to the fenced-in backyard. It was a little weird to not go through the fence.

I hadn't been on the trampoline since that day Teddy caught me alone. It was strange being here with anyone but the Swift boys. This was our place, after all. It might have been Teddy's trampoline, but sharing it with him felt strange. Almost wrong.

We bounced together for a while, and I tried to smile and laugh. But it was hard. It got harder, too, when his parents came out the back door.

"Don't mind us," Mrs. Ryan said. "We're just getting the yard picked up."

"Do you know how to play Popcorn?" Teddy asked me. "You can be the kernel first, if you want?"

"Um . . . okay."

But I was too busy watching Mr. and Mrs. Ryan to pay much attention. Mr. Ryan had just started going around the edge of the yard, pulling up weeds. He stopped, crouched near the edge of the fence. He leaned on a board for support.

On *the* board.

"Oh, looks like I'll have to fix this," he said.

"Fix what?" Mrs. Ryan asked.

"The fence. There's a loose board."

I started to feel choked up and coughed into my elbow to hide it. Teddy stared at me. I think he knew. I think he could tell that hearing that — hearing that the fence was getting fixed — upset me. It was stupid. The boys and I hadn't even been here together all summer. Not since the last day of school.

But knowing that we *couldn't* anymore . . . Just like finding out that the wedding was the day of the circus, it felt like more than it actually was. It felt like I was losing more than this trampoline. It felt a lot bigger. A lot more painful.

"I need to go home," I told Teddy.

"You just got here, though," he said.

"I know. I'm sorry. I ain't feeling well."

"Okay," he said, even though I could tell he was kinda sad. "Do you want me to walk you home?"

I shook my head. "I'll be all right. Thanks for having me over."

When I got home, I stood in my driveway and just stared at the Swifts' half of the duplex. The blinds were shut, so I couldn't see inside, but I knew all the boys were there, so I just pretended I was inside with them. I imagined that everything was the same as it had been at the start of the summer. Brian was going to parties with girls and blushing when we asked about kissing. Kevin jabbering about everything. And Canaan gave me a gap-toothed smile.

I pretended I wasn't going nowhere and that things could stay like that forever.

But it couldn't. I could only pretend for so long.

The fact was, things had changed. And they were just gonna keep changing, whether I wanted them to or not.

Richard's truck pulled into the driveway a second later. "Hey, kiddo," he said, climbing out of the front seat. "I just went to the grocery store. What do you say you and me surprise your mama with dinner tonight?"

I tore my eyes away from the Swifts' windows and looked at Richard. For the first time, I wasn't happy to see him. My chest felt heavy. Like there was a brick inside instead of a heart.

"Did you hear me, kiddo?" Richard asked.

"Yeah," I mumbled. "Dinner. Sure, I'll help."

# Chapter Nineteen

The wedding was coming up on us fast, and I was keeping busy helping Mama and Richard get everything ready. We'd also started moving a few things into our new house. Mama wanted the house ready so we could start living there right after the wedding.

"Are y'all going on a honeymoon?" I asked her.

She laughed. "The new house is our honeymoon," she said. "I'd take moving out of this duplex over a week in Hawaii any day."

I didn't say nothing, but I thought she was crazy. Whenever I got married, I was going to Hawaii for sure. Or maybe California. Somewhere with a lot of sun and a beach. I'd never seen the ocean before.

Canaan came over while I was packing one afternoon. His lip was still swollen and his eye was a little bruised, but he looked better for the most part. "Hey," he said, sitting down on my bed.

"Hey."

It felt weird having Canaan in my room again after all this time. I always thought that once he stopped being a jerk, things would just go back to normal. That I'd be happy. But I wasn't, exactly. I didn't know what I felt.

"Packing?" he asked.

I nodded.

"Wow. I can't believe you're really moving. You won't be next door anymore. Is the house real big? Do you like it?"

"It's nice," I said. Canaan was here, like I'd wished for all summer, and I didn't want him to leave. But at the same time, I didn't want him to stay. It hurt both ways.

"It's real pretty outside," he said. "The Ryans ain't home. Wanna go jump on the trampoline?"

"We can't," I said. "They got the fence fixed." I thought he might get mad about this. Blame me for it. And even though he didn't, that I'd even have to worry about that now made *me* mad. "Oh. That sucks.

What about Rocky's? It's kinda hot. Wanna go get milkshakes?"

"I can't. I need to stay here and pack."

"Maybe when you're done?"

"No," I murmured. I wanted to say yes, I really did, but I couldn't. There was something bubbling in my chest, something that had been there for the whole summer, simmering, and the way Canaan was looking at me right now, like nothing had happened at all, was about to make it explode.

"Why?" he asked. "Are you busy later, too?"

"No!" I said, the volcano in my chest finally erupting. "No, Canaan, I'm not busy, but I can't go to Rocky's with you. Or to the playground. Or none of that. You've been awful to me all summer! You've made fun of me and said real mean things to me and maybe you helped me yesterday with Andy and Peter, but you let them kick me a few times first."

"Nola —"

"No," I said again. My hands were shaking and I felt sick. I didn't yell at people. Especially not my best-best friend. But I couldn't hold it in no more. And I couldn't let him pretend nothing had happened after the way he'd treated me for months. "I was there for you — I was a good friend to you when you needed me. Even though you kept pushing me away. But I needed you this summer, too, and you weren't there and you were a jerk. You picked Andy and Peter over me. You spray-painted Mrs. Santos's mailbox and hurt Felicia's *puppy*. And probably worse. You were a different Canaan, and I didn't like him at all."

He got real quiet. I took a deep breath and tried to calm down. My heart was beating real fast. All I could do was stare at him. At this boy who had been my best friend. Until he wasn't. Like his pain was so big he hadn't seen me, here, wanting to help.

"I'm sorry," he finally said. "Nola, I mean it. I am. Can't we just go back to the way things were?" He was staring down at his sneakers, not looking at me.

"No." I shook my head. "I don't think we can. At least, not right away." I swallowed the lump rising in my throat. All summer I'd wanted this — the old Canaan, the way things used to be — but now that it was in front of me, I didn't want it no more. Not like this. "I . . . I have a lot to do. I think you oughta go."

"Nola." His voice was sad, pitiful even. He looked up. Looked at me. But I still didn't know what to say to him. I almost didn't recognize him. Even if he was acting like the old Canaan now, I couldn't forget the mean, harsh boy he'd been all summer. I couldn't see him the same way no more.

"I'll see you at the wedding."

He stood up and walked to my bedroom door. He looked one last time, and I thought maybe he was about to cry, too. "I'm real sorry," he said again. Then he left and I sat on my floor, face in my hands, and bawled like a baby.

*  *  *

Later that night, I was sitting up in bed, drawing a picture of Mama in her wedding dress. I'd been drawing all evening, ever since Canaan left. It was the only thing that could make me feel better. I had to focus on my hands and the lines my pencil was making too much to think about him.

Mama tapped on my door and stuck her head in. "Hey," she said. "The tea I made earlier is cold now. You want me to get you a glass?"

"Sure."

She left for the kitchen and returned a minute later, a mason jar in each hand. She gave one to me and I took a big, long drink. I loved Mama's tea. She made it sweeter than most people, and that was saying something where we were from. Richard always said it was more sugar than tea. I liked it that way, though.

"So," she said, sitting down on the edge of the bed and looking around my room. "Looks like you got a lot of packing done today."

I nodded.

"How you feeling?" she asked. "About moving, I mean. I know you weren't too thrilled about it earlier this summer."

"I . . . I don't know," I said. "I'm not as sad about it now."

"Because of how things are going with Canaan?"

I looked up at her, surprised.

"I heard y'all in here earlier," she admitted. "And I knew this had been a rough summer for both of you. I didn't want to bring it up too much — I figured if you wanted to talk about it you would, but . . ."

"You've been so busy with the wedding," I said. "I didn't want to burden you."

"Oh, Nola Baby, you never burden me. I just thought you needed space to figure it out for yourself." She reached out and touched my cheek. "You are the most important part of my life. You always come first. Do you wanna talk about it now? I'm all yours."

I closed my sketchpad and set it aside. "Mama, I've spent all summer wanting Canaan back. We've been fighting for months. But today, when he was here . . . I was so mad. And I just . . . I'm scared I'm gonna be like Grandma Lucy. That losing Canaan is gonna leave me an angry, mean person."

"Sweetheart," Mama murmured.

"How did you do it?" I asked. "How did you deal with losing Daddy? You didn't turn mean and angry."

"Well, I did at first," she said. "I was real angry for a while. Sometimes I still am. But I realized that, even though I lost your daddy, I had other good things. Like you. You kept me strong."

"But Grandma Lucy —"

"Grandma Lucy has had a harder time dealing with her pain," Mama said. "Some people do. But you're not Grandma Lucy, Nola. And you haven't really lost Canaan. He was here today, wasn't he?"

"Yeah, but . . . he's different. I don't know if I can ever be friends with him like I used to be."

"I understand," Mama said. "I always thought you two would work it out. But you're only twelve. There will be other best friends. That doesn't mean you can't miss Canaan, but I don't think you have to worry about being angry forever, either. And like I said, you haven't lost him. He might not be your best friend now, but he's still here."

I looked down at my hands, folded in my lap. "I wish this summer never happened."

"You mean that?" Mama asked. "Seems like some good things happened. Teddy seems like a good friend. If this summer never happened, y'all might not have gotten close."

I smiled a little, thinking of Teddy. She was right. A lot of bad had happened this summer, but there was good, too.

"Well, I think it's time for bed. At least for me." She kissed me on the forehead and stood up. "Don't be up to late, okay?"

"I won't. Good night, Mama."

"Good night, Nola Baby." She looked back over her shoulder before walking out of my room. "And, hey, remember, you're allowed to be angry at him. It doesn't mean you'll be mad forever. I promise. It'll get better."

"Thanks, Mama."

She nodded and slipped out the door, closing it quietly behind her.

*   *   *

I left a note on Teddy Ryan's front porch the next day. *Meet me at noon in the woods behind my house*, it said. *Bring an old sheet.*

When I first got there and he hadn't shown up yet, I was worried. Maybe he didn't get the note. Or maybe he was busy. I really should've called, but leaving a note felt more mysterious. I'd never really been mysterious before, and all of a sudden, I wanted to. It was exciting.

Teddy showed up just a couple minutes after twelve, a baby-blue sheet folded up under his arm. "Sorry I'm late," he said. "I had to find a sheet my parents would let me out of the house with."

"That's okay," I said. "I would've brought one, but almost all our stuff is packed up now."

He pointed at the grocery bag I was carrying. "What's in there?"

"You'll see. Come on. Follow me."

I led him through the woods, weaving between trees

and hopping over fallen branches. Teddy was always a few steps behind me, stumbling a little. When I looked back, his khakis were covered with grass and dirt. I felt a little guilty.

"We're almost there," I told him just as the trees started to give way. A second later, we were standing in a little clearing, if you could even call it that. It wasn't a big space, but it was pretty. A stretch of tall green grass surrounded by trees. I'd been here a million times over the years, making up imaginary worlds with Canaan and Brian and Kevin. But it was the first time I'd been here all summer.

"Wow," Teddy said behind me.

"Pretty, huh?"

He nodded. "I ain't been out here before."

"Really?"

"No. I've always stayed in my backyard mostly. I've always been scared of getting lost."

"The woods ain't that big," I told him. "It's hard to get lost."

He looked down at his feet, like he was embarrassed. So I changed the subject right quick.

"As many times as I've been out here, I ain't never had a picnic," I explained. "Always wanted to, but Kevin's always been real scared of bugs getting in his food and . . . well, we just never did it. But now that I'm moving, I thought this was my last chance, and I thought it'd be fun to have a picnic with you."

He looked back up, and now he was grinning. Really, really grinning. "All right," he said. "A picnic sounds nice."

I stepped aside and let him spread out the blanket. I'd actually gotten the idea to do this last night, after Mama reminded me why not all this summer was bad. Teddy was one of the best parts of the summer, and I wanted to spend a little more time with him before I moved.

"I'm sorry I left in such a hurry the other day," I told him, sitting down on the sheet. "When we were on the trampoline. That was rude of me."

"No big deal," Teddy said. "I'm sorry my parents fixed the fence."

"It was bound to happen sooner or later." I opened up the grocery bag and started pulling out the food I'd brought. "I made you a sandwich. It's mostly just vegetables, so I hope you aren't allergic to anything on it."

"Thanks," he said, taking the sandwich bag I'd handed him.

We started eating, not saying a whole lot. I was

feeling a little nervous, but I wasn't really sure why. It only got worse, too, when Teddy pointed to the grocery bag. "What else is in there?"

"Oh, um . . . well, I brought you something." I took out my sketchpad and flipped to a drawing near the middle. It was a drawing of Teddy, one I'd been working on since the day at the mall. Right before I showed him, all sorts of worries ran through my head. What if he hated it? What if he thought it was weird that I'd drawn him? What if he made fun of me?

But Teddy took the sketchpad from my hand and looked down and smiled, and that made me smile back.

"Is this me?" he asked.

"Yep."

He laughed. "And I'm eating cake in the picture."

"A big piece," I told him. "I figured if you can't eat cake in real life, might as well get to in a drawing."

He looked up at me, still grinning. "It's real good, Nola. You're really a good drawer."

My face heated up and I had to look away. I always felt embarrassed when people complimented me, but somehow, coming from Teddy, it was different. I felt even more shy, but it felt good, too. It was hard to explain.

"Can I keep the picture?" he asked.

"Sure. If you want."

He pulled the page out of the sketchpad very, very carefully, like he was scared of ripping the edges. "I'll put it up in my room," he said. "Like Felicia did with the picture of JW."

"You don't gotta."

"I want to."

I started blushing again.

The rest of the picnic was real nice. We finished our sandwiches and just sat there for a while, talking and laughing until clouds started to stretch across the sky, hiding the sun from our view. We packed up, worried it might rain, and trudged back through the woods to my backyard.

"Thanks for the sandwich," Teddy said. "And the drawing. And for the picnic. It was fun."

"Yeah, it was. . . . I'm gonna be busy helping Mama with stuff for the next few days, but I'll see you at the wedding, right?"

"Yep. Me and my parents will be there."

"Good. See you around, Teddy."

I walked inside the house, feeling happier than I had all summer.

# Chapter Twenty

I didn't see Canaan or the other boys again until the wedding, when I was walking down the aisle of the church, ahead of Mama, wearing my new dress. I'd been staring at myself in the mirror almost all morning. I didn't mean to be vain, but I'd had my hair done that morning — pulled back in a sleek bun with curls down, framing my face — and I even had a little makeup on. Between that and the coral dress, I felt *pretty*. Prettier than I'd ever felt or looked before. And older. So walking down the middle of the church, with everyone watching, I felt a little like a celebrity. Even if Mama was the real star.

I spotted all three of the Swift brothers and their mama sitting in one of the pews. The boys were in khakis and button-down shirts, and Mrs. Swift was wearing a real pretty floral dress. It was the first time I'd seen her all summer, and all I could think was how tired she looked, even when she smiled at me.

When Mama came down the aisle in that dress she'd hunted so hard for, she looked beautiful. She looked more like she was floating than walking, like an angel, and she had on the biggest smile I'd ever seen. All those weeks of panicking and stress disappeared like that.

Richard seemed happy, too. He stared at Mama like she was the prettiest thing he'd ever seen — and she probably was. When she reached him and they were standing next to each other, it was like none of the rest of us were there. Like they could only see each other.

The preacher led them through their vows, and Mama and Richard repeated, sometimes stumbling and laughing like little kids. I laughed, too.

But then, when they said "I do," something hit me, and I couldn't help feeling a little nervous.

"What's the matter, kiddo?" Richard asked me during the reception. The DJ had just announced the father-daughter dance and he'd come over to find me sitting at an empty table. "You seem down."

"I'm all right."

"Come on now," he said, leading me onto the dance floor as a Tim McGraw song started up through the speakers. "I can tell something's bothering you."

It was hard to dance with Richard, him being so tall and all. He had to slump forward and I had to reach my arms up high. Across the room, I could see Mama standing alone. She was still smiling, still happy, but she didn't have a father to dance with. We'd always been left out at other people's weddings. Always the ones standing by ourselves. But for the first time, I had someone to dance with during the father-daughter dance. I should've been happy, but really, I was scared.

"Promise you'll say good-bye," I said to Richard. "If you and Mama ever split up, promise you'll at least say good-bye, okay?"

"Hey, where is this coming from?" he asked. "Wait . . . I'm sure I know. Nola." He stopped dancing and knelt down in front of me, the way you might with a kid half my age. It was the only way for him to look me in the eye. "Listen to me. I don't ever plan on leaving. I love you and your mama so, so much. But, if for some reason this doesn't work out, you have nothing to worry about."

"What do you mean?"

He put a hand on my shoulder. "I mean that I'll always be your stepdad, even if I'm not with your mama anymore. I'll always be a part of your life if you want me to be. Understood?"

I nodded.

Richard pulled me in for a tight hug. "Don't worry," he said before he'd even let me go. "I'm not going anywhere."

We finished the dance, then Mama was calling us over for pictures. We posed in front of the photographer a bunch of times. I got my picture taken with everybody in our family, but I think my favorite was the picture Mama asked for — one of her, me, and Grandma Lucy together.

I looked up at Grandma Lucy, and for once, she smiled at me. I think we were both thinking the same thing: This would've been a great picture for the collage we'd made together.

But the smile started to slip when I remembered about Grandpa's drill. Grandma Lucy had never brought it up, which meant she hadn't noticed yet. But I felt bad. Like I was lying. I knew I might be in trouble when she found out, and it scared me. I'd always had Canaan to do this stuff for me, to protect me, but now I had to start standing up for myself, taking responsibility.

"Grandma Lucy," I said once we'd stepped away and the photographer started taking pictures of Richard's family. "I gotta tell you something."

"What's that?" she asked.

"I . . . I, um . . ." I swallowed. I had to tell her, even if it meant she'd yell. I might've looked older in the mirror earlier, but I had to act older, too. "When I was cleaning the garage, I started listening to music and dancing around — and I know I shouldn't have been goofing off and I didn't mean no harm by it, but . . . I fell and hit the workbench and some of Grandpa's tools . . . well, a couple fell, and the drill . . ."

Grandma Lucy was staring at me. Staring hard in a way that made my stomach jump all over the place.

"The drill broke," I said finally. "I'm so sorry. I didn't mean to. I know you're probably mad —"

"I ain't mad."

At first I wasn't sure I'd heard her right. "You're not?"

She sighed and shook her head. "Not at you. I'm upset the drill is broken, but I've been thinking a lot since we did that collage for your mama. I ain't touched those tools in years. But they can't bring him back. I'm sad, but I'm not mad at you."

I was in shock. I'd expected yelling. Lots of yelling. But she wasn't even mad at me. The look on her face, though, those sad eyes wet with tears, might've been worse. I wondered if that's how I'd looked all summer.

"I'm sorry," I said again. "I know I should've told you sooner, but I was so worried you'd get mad."

"Yes, you should've told me, but . . . it's just a drill, Fionnula. A very old drill."

That wasn't what I was sorry about this time, though. I stepped forward and gave Grandma Lucy a hug. She patted my back twice, then cleared her throat. "All right, then. That's enough. We oughta go back to the reception."

"Okay," I said, taking a step back.

"Thank you, though," she said. "For telling me the truth. That was very . . . very brave of you. I know I ain't the easiest person to . . . Well, anyway. Thank you."

I was headed back to the reception when I bumped into Mr. Briggs in the hallway. "Nola," he said. "Just who I was hoping to see. Mrs. Hooper is about to drive me home, but I had to give you something first."

"Give me something?" I asked.

He nodded. "I left it in the pile of wedding presents since I couldn't find you. You'll know which one is yours. I didn't wrap it."

"Mr. Briggs, that's real nice of you, but it's Mama and Richard's wedding day. They're the ones you oughta be giving presents to," I said.

He chuckled. "It's nothing special," he said. "Just something I thought you might like."

"Well, thank you," I said. "You really didn't have to —"

He waved a withered, old hand. "Don't you worry about it. Enjoy the rest of your day."

"You too, Mr. Briggs."

I headed back into the reception hall, where everybody was eating and dancing. I was about to go looking for Mr. Briggs's present when I heard someone clear their throat behind me. I turned around and saw Teddy Ryan standing there, dressed in a suit.

"Hey," I said, feeling a smile spread across my face "You look nice."

"Thank you," he said. "You look real pretty."

I blushed. "So what's up?" I asked.

"Nothing," he said. "I just — uh — here." He shoved something into my hand — a tiny piece of paper — then he stepped back real quick. "Read it, and think about it."

"Um, okay."

"Okay."

And just like that, he turned around and hurried back to the table where his parents were sitting. I sat down in a chair and carefully unfolded Teddy's note.

Dear Nola,

I'm real glad we got to be friends this summer. It's been a lot of fun. Do you want to be my girlfriend? Or at least sit with me at lunch when school starts since I'll be in the middle school with you now? Hope so. Talk to you soon.

Teddy

I had to read it a couple times to realize what it said. Teddy Ryan liked me? Like, he wanted to be my boyfriend? I was surprised, but I guess I shouldn't have been.

He had almost held my hand while we watched the fireworks, after all.

I didn't know how I felt about it, though. I definitely liked Teddy more now than I had at the beginning of the summer — he really was sweet and we got along real well. He was my friend. My good friend, actually. I'd just never thought of him being anything more than that. I'd never thought of anyone being more than that. Except Canaan, maybe.

Now, with the way everything had changed, the whole idea of marrying Canaan one day seemed kinda stupid and babyish.

But Teddy . . . I just didn't know.

I decided I'd definitely sit with him at lunch on the first day of school, and by then I'd have an answer for him about the boyfriend thing. I hope he didn't mind waiting that long.

I'd just tucked the note into my tiny silver purse when Canaan came walking toward me from across the room. He looked real nice in his dress pants and button-down shirt. His hair was fixed, and his lip had healed. He looked better than I'd seen him all summer, actually.

"Hey," he said, sounding nervous. "That, um, that was a nice wedding."

"Yeah. It was."

He shifted, shoving his hands in his pockets. "You look pretty. I like your hair like that."

I touched the bun Mama had done that morning. There were about a million bobby pins shoved in it, holding my curls in place, and it was stiff with hairspray. But it did look pretty. And I couldn't help feeling glad Canaan had noticed, even if I was still kinda uneasy around him. "Thank you," I said.

"You're welcome. . . . You, uh, you wanna dance?" he asked.

"Um . . . sure. All right."

We were both nervous. I put my hands on his shoulders and his were on my waist, but neither of us could quite manage to look each other in the eye. He kept stepping on my toes and I kept tripping on his feet.

"Sorry," we both mumbled at least ten times before he finally started talking.

"So . . . is Teddy Ryan your boyfriend now?" he asked.

I blushed. "Maybe. I don't know. Why? Are you going to make fun of me again for being friends with him?"

"No," he said quickly. "I'm not. I'm sorry I did before. I was just . . . It was weird seeing you hang out with him. Like he was your best friend now and I wasn't no more."

"Well, you weren't really around and you stopped talking to me," I reminded him. "I wasn't sure we were best friends."

"I know. I'm sorry." He chewed on the inside of his cheek for a second. "I've been mad a lot. Ever since *he* left. I've been mad at everybody. I'm still mad, but when Andy and Peter knocked you down, that made me mad in a different way. Made me realize what a jerk I'd been, acting like them. I'm sorry."

"I know you are," I said. Because I knew he was, but that didn't mean it was all okay now. Truth was, I didn't know if I'd be able to see Canaan the same way again. I wasn't angry at him anymore — I'd kinda got that out of my system when I yelled at him in my bedroom the other day — but we'd never be the kind of friends we used to be. "But I ain't sure that's enough. Everything's changed now, you know?"

He nodded, but he looked heartbroken. "I know. I shouldn't have done what I did. Even if I was mad, you were my best friend. I shouldn't have been mad at you. And, like you said, I should've been there when you needed me this summer, too."

I didn't know what else to say, so I just nodded and kept dancing. Even though my heart hurt.

"My dad messed everything up," he said.

"Yeah," I agreed. "He did."

I didn't care what Brian said. Canaan needed to know the truth about why Mr. Swift had left. He deserved to know where his daddy was. It wasn't fair for him to be left in the dark, always wondering. I had to tell him what I'd found out.

"About your daddy," I said.

Canaan looked down at his feet. "It's stupid," he said. "I know he's not coming back. I know he's gone, but sometimes I make up reasons for why in my head. You know, like . . . like I pretend he was really a secret agent and he had to leave to go spy on some other country. Stuff like that."

It did sound stupid. And silly.

Kinda like my dreams of growing up to marry Canaan and live next door to Brian and Kevin. Stupid and silly, but safe. Happy. Better than the truth.

Maybe Brian was right. Maybe it was better to let Canaan make up stories in his head for now. Maybe the truth would be more of a burden than a relief. I remembered what Mr. Briggs had told me on his front porch — that no one wants to grow up. Canaan would find out about Mr. Swift and Sarah Clarke eventually, but for now, maybe I oughta just let him have his childish hopes.

"It's possible," I lied.

Canaan smiled, showing off the gap between his teeth. Then he stepped on my toe so hard that I yelped.

"Sorry," he said. "I guess I'm not a great dancer."

"You guessed right," I said. "No wonder you never go to the dances at school. You'd break every girl's toes off."

He laughed. It was the first time I'd heard him laugh all summer, and it couldn't have sounded better.

# Five Summers Ago

*Canaan's laugh was the only thing I could hear, hot and loud and rippling right in my ear. We were sitting on the back of a ginormous elephant, and Canaan was behind me, his head right over my shoulder, his mouth right by my ear. I was laughing, too. We were on an elephant! An elephant!*

*"Was that fun?" Mama asked as she helped me and Canaan down and the next kids in line stepped up to the big gray animal.*

*"Can we go again?" Canaan asked. "Please?"*

*"Maybe," Mrs. Swift said. "But we have other things to get to first. Kevin wants to see the lions."*

*"Rawr!" Kevin hollered. He was sitting on his mama's hip, though he was just a tiny bit too big to do that now. "Rawr! Lions! Rawr!"*

*"Where's Brian?" I asked.*

*"His dad took him to buy a glow stick," Mama said. "I told him to get one for all of you."*

*"Yes!" Canaan and me both shouted. Everybody in the arena had a glow stick or a glow necklace, and we'd both been wanting them since we got to the circus. Mrs. Swift and Mama laughed.*

"Come on," Mama said. "Time to go see the lions. You know you can have your picture taken with the baby ones, right?"

So a second later me and Canaan were sitting together, a baby lion between us. The lion cub licked my fingers, and his tongue was rough like a regular cat's was. It tickled.

We did everything there was to do that day — except go watch the clowns. I didn't like clowns much. By the time we were on our way home, we were all real tired.

"This was the best day ever," Canaan said.

"Yeah," I agreed.

"We have to come again when the circus comes back to Besser County."

"Definitely. Kevin was too little to do everything this time. We have to bring him."

"Of course," Canaan said. "But I think we should come every time it comes back. Even when we get bigger and stuff."

"Like, even when we're sixty?" I asked.

"Even when we're seventy," he said. "Or a hundred. We won't never be too old for this. And we'll always come together. No matter what."

I nodded and leaned my head on his shoulder. We were in the backseat of Mama's car — the other boys had ridden back with the Swifts — and I was having a hard time keeping my eyes open. I think Canaan was, too, because his voice started fading in and out, like he was dozing off.

"Best . . . day ever," he said again. "And it'll be just as fun next time. Maybe . . . maybe better."

# Chapter Twenty-One

We packed up the last of our things the next morning. Mama and Richard had everything loaded into the back of his truck and the trunk of her car by noon, then Richard went on to the new house while Mama met with Mr. Harker, our landlord, so he could make sure there was no damage or anything inside our half of the duplex.

I stood outside with the Swifts. Mrs. Swift kept telling me over and over how much they'd miss Mama and me. She didn't seem much like her old self. She was quieter. And she seemed a little blue. But other than that, she looked all right. All the boys did, too. I guess Brian's talk with them about getting things back together had worked.

Maybe they weren't okay just yet, but they would be.

"I can't believe you're leaving," Canaan said. "You've always been here. It'll be weird not having you next door."

"I know."

"Y'all will still see each other at school," Mrs. Swift reminded us. "It starts next week. You'll probably be in the same homeroom and everything."

We nodded, but I think we both knew it wasn't the same. Who knew how often we'd see each other at school? Even if we were in the same classes, it wouldn't be like before. Especially since I'd decided to start eating lunch with Teddy.

Kevin reached out and squeezed my hand. I knew that was his way of saying that *he* wouldn't see me in school. He was still in elementary school. And Brian was going into high school. I wouldn't see either of them hardly at all after today. Just the thought made me choke up. Sure, Canaan had been my best-best friend, but the other boys had been my best friends, too.

"Good-bye, Mr. Harker," Mama was saying as she stepped out of our front door for the last time. "Have a nice day." She turned to me. "Ready to go, Nola Baby?"

I nodded.

Mrs. Swift gave Mama a hug. "Congratulations, again," she said. "And if you ever need anything, you know who to call."

"Thanks, Debbie," she said. "Same to you. Bye, boys. I'll miss having y'all around for dinner — I don't know what I'll do with all the extra food."

I went through and gave each of the boys a hug, starting with Brian. He squeezed me tight for a second, then let me go slowly. Canaan was next. Even though I knew he'd miss me the most, our hug was quick and awkward. Kinda like our dancing. Kinda like everything between us now.

Last was Kevin. He wrapped his short, chubby arms around my neck so hard that he nearly pulled me down. And then, just when I was about to pull away, he whispered, "I'll miss you, Nola."

Four words. The first words he'd said all summer.

I wanted to scream and holler and tell everyone. I wanted to celebrate. He was talking again! But I knew that he'd whispered for a reason. Those words were just for me. His good-bye present. When he was ready to share with everyone else, he would.

"I'll miss you, too," I whispered back.

"Come on," Mama said, putting a hand on my shoulder. "Richard's waiting on us."

"Bye," I said, waving over my shoulder as I followed her to the car. They waved back. They waved and kept waving right up until our car turned the corner out of the subdivision.

That was the same time I finally started to cry.

"Oh, baby," Mama said, taking a hand off the gearshift and putting it on my knee. She didn't say nothing else. She didn't tell me it was going to be okay or that I'd see them again soon. She just let me cry for a few minutes.

I wasn't just losing the boys, I realized. I was ending an entire part of my life. A part that had lasted as long as I could remember, where I was Nola, the Swift brothers' best friend and next-door neighbor. Now a new part of my life was about to start, and I didn't know what was ahead for me. It was exciting, but also kinda scary.

"Look," Mama said, pointing out the window. "Yard sale. Think we oughta stop in and check it out?"

I nodded and wiped the tears of my face with the back of my hand.

"All right," she said. "Maybe we can find some cool stuff for the new house."

I saw the trampoline as soon as Mama stopped the car. It was the exact same as Teddy Ryan's, only this one had a For Sale sign sitting right on top of it. I went straight over to it while Mama wandered around the yard checking out the other things up for grabs.

"We can deliver that, too."

I turned and saw a man sitting in a lawn chair. He gave me a big smile.

"My kids loved that trampoline. Ain't used it in years, though. Guess they outgrew it. If y'all want to buy it, I can take it wherever you want in my truck. Delivery free of charge."

"Really?"

He nodded.

"Trampoline, huh?" Mama said, coming back over to me. She looked at the price on the For Sale sign. "Well, you do have all that money you saved up this summer if you want to buy it."

That's when the idea hit me. I'd been putting off using most of that saved money, holding out on the hope of going to the circus. Now that it had passed, I had to find something just as good to spend the money on. I remembered Teddy's parents fixing the broken board in the fence, closing up mine and the boys' secret place.

"I'll take it," I said.

"Great," the man in the lawn chair said. He got to his feet. "Let me get a notebook and you can write down where I oughta take it to."

Mama smiled at me. "This will be great in the backyard at the new house," she said.

"It ain't for me," I told her.

She raised an eyebrow. "No?"

I shook my head, and when the man came back with the notebook, I wrote down the address of the duplex. The Swifts' address. This was for them.

I was putting stuff away in my new room a few hours later when Mama knocked on the door. "Hey," she said. "I was going through the wedding gifts and I found this. Pretty sure it's for you." She held out a small wooden figurine.

"Oh! Mr. Briggs!" I grabbed it from her. "He told me he'd left something for me at the wedding, but I forgot."

"Well, take a look," she said. "I think you'll like it."

I held up the wooden statue so I could see it a little better. This one was bigger than most I'd seen, and I realized that's because it was a carving of four different people, all standing real close to each other.

There was a tall boy with glasses. A short, tiny boy with lots of hair. Then, in the middle, a boy and girl. The girl was a little chubby with a curly ponytail, and the boy had a friendly arm thrown around her.

"Isn't it beautiful?" Mama said. "It's you and Canaan and Brian and Kevin. That is the best I've ever seen Mr. Briggs do on one of these. You oughta send him a thank-you note."

"I will," I said. "Definitely."

"He's the sweetest man," she said. "That was so nice of him."

I nodded.

Richard hollered for her from the living room. "Can you help me carry the entertainment center in?"

"Coming!" Mama called.

She left me alone in my new room, still staring at the little statue Mr. Briggs had given me. I ran my fingers over all the tiny wooden faces. They were all smiling.

I put it on the table next to my bed, a place I'd always be able to see it.

No matter what happened with me and the Swift boys after that summer — whether we stayed friends or drifted further apart, no matter who I ended up married to or who lived next door to them — at least this version of us would always be together.

# Acknowledgments

I could have never written this book without many helpful hands, and, as Nola would say, it'd be awful rude not to thank them.

Thank you to Joanna Volpe, who has always offered outstanding advice and encouragement, even when I might have seemed a little crazy. Thanks for always having faith. And to Jody Corbett, who brought out the best parts of Nola and the boys and who made me see Teddy in a completely new way. Thanks for that, Jody. And also for letting me babble about my dog sometimes (all the time) when you were helping me brainstorm.

A huge thanks must go to everyone at New Leaf Literary and Scholastic. There are far too many of you to name here, but I appreciate each and every one of you and the ways you've helped to make Nola's story come alive.

Thanks to Phoebe North and Lisa Desrochers — two of the best friends and writers I've ever known. Thank you for the endless support and advice. I'd be lost without you both.

Thanks to Molly and Shana, my real-life best friends. No matter how we drift apart, we'll always come back together in the end.

Thanks to my parents, my siblings, my grandparents and aunts and uncles and cousins — I could never do this without your love and support. I'm lucky to have each and every one of you in my life.

And thanks to McLean County, my hometown, and all the stories it has given me. I can't imagine the person I'd be if I'd grown up anywhere else. No matter where I go, I'll never forget where I came from. There would be no Nola, no Swift boys, no story here without that little town in western Kentucky.

# About the Author

Kody Keplinger was born and raised in rural western Kentucky. She always enjoyed writing and began working on "novels" when she was eleven. She wrote her first published young-adult work during her senior year of high school and hasn't stopped writing novels ever since. *The Swift Boys & Me* is Kody's middle-grade debut. She currently lives in New York City and writes full-time.